Once In Another World

ONCE IN ANOTHER
WORLD

Brendan John Sweeney

NEW ISLAND

ONCE IN ANOTHER WORLD
First published 2013
by New Island
2 Brookside
Dundrum Road
Dublin 14

www.newisland.ie

PRINT ISBN: 978-184840-233-1
EPUB ISBN: 978-184840-234-8
MOBI ISBN: 978-184840-235-5

Typeset by JVR Creative India
Cover design by Inga Thorunn Waage.
Printed by TJ International Ltd,Padstow, Cornwall

New Island received financial assistance from
The Arts Council (An Comhairle Ealaíon), Dublin, Ireland

10 9 8 7 6 5 4 3 2 1

1

Dublin: half past two in the morning, 27 March 1937.
Holland stood in the shadow of a doorway.

The wind was bitter and his eyes watered as they
scanned the empty street. A hailstorm, an hour previously, had filled the spaces between the cobblestones
with tiny beads of ice, and they glittered in the slanted
light of the streetlamps. Mixed in with the wind was the
plaintive lowing of the cattle from the livestock market
off the North Circular Road.

Holland pulled his heavy greatcoat about him and
walked briskly through the darkened streets towards the
river.

McDaid was waiting for him in front of the Irish
Press offices on Burgh Quay. His hat was pulled low and
he gripped his collar tightly to his neck. A newspaper van
spluttered into life on the other side of the river.

"This is a strange place to meet, Commandant," said
Holland.

"I have my reasons. You weren't followed?"

Holland shook his head.

"These are hard times for the Movement. We don't
want to lose you because of a touch of carelessness, do we?"

Holland's eyes followed the white edge of the water
as it lapped against the quayside.

"To be honest, I didn't think anyone really gave a
damn about me any more."

"No self-pity now. You'd be surprised how highly you're regarded."

Holland looked as if nothing could surprise him. He looked tense though. His years in the Movement had taken their toll. His head moved slightly from side to side, his eyes strained to collect the maximum amount of information from his field of vision. There was no one watching as far as he could see, but he wondered why McDaid had chosen such a spot to meet. It felt wrong.

McDaid read his anxiety. "Take it easy, man. I chose this time because of Broy's Special Branch thugs. There's a gap in their shifts. The lazy bastards get a couple of hours' extra sleep from two till five, all on Free State overtime. Anyone who sees us here will take us for printers from the Press offices. I know the names of a few fellas in there if we're asked."

Holland continued to stare at the borrowed light on the surface of the Liffey.

"What do you want me to do, Commandant?"

McDaid moved closer: Holland caught the smell of stale tobacco on his breath.

"The Movement is in a mess. HQ hasn't a clue what to do. Nothing but spouting about raids on post offices and banks. And all it will do is bleed us of our best men." McDaid spat over the embankment. "I'll tell you something but you have to keep it under your hat—," he looked up, "if you ever bothered wearing one, that is. We may be able to get our hands on some really big money. It will get us back into gear in the North."

Holland looked sceptical. "To be honest, I've had enough of hanging around here waiting for campaigns that never get off the drawing board, always being told we're 'on the verge'. I'm thinking of volunteering for Spain."

McDaid's eyes burned and he turned to face Holland directly for the first time.

"Don't go *there*," he hissed. "Take it from me, it's nothing but a sideshow and they don't need more clowns." He drew in a deep breath. "I have something for you, something you'll enjoy—it's a driving job."

"Bank or post office?" asked Holland cynically.

"Enough joking. You'll be a chauffeur. Your boss is a foreign businessman. From Hungary."

"I don't want a job, I want to go to Spain. Your generation got their fill after the Rising. Now it's our turn."

"Patience, patience. That will come, but we need you in this job. It's important. You're to drive this Hungarian fella around the city. It pays four quid a week."

Holland whistled. "That's good money for just a driving job."

"There is more to it than just driving. You're to keep an eye on him as well. You'll need a gun."

"Hold on! You want me to risk a couple of years in Arbour Hill for a civilian job?"

"It's all been arranged. The gun is registered in his name and he has a licence. All you'll have to do is keep it in the car. It's as simple as that. Think of it; you'll have some money in your pocket and you'll be well rested before we start the next campaign. What do you say?" McDaid pressed Holland's arm. "You can always quit if it doesn't suit you."

McDaid stared up at the younger man. His eyes were watery from the cold. He made Holland think of a very old, very clever dog.

"What about my motor licence? The name's a give-away."

"We can arrange that. Just steer clear of the constabulary for the first few days."

"All right, I'll give it a try."

"Good."

"Do you have an address for this Hungarian character?"

"All in good time. The gun's a Parabellum. There are two magazines, eight rounds in each. I've been trying to get rid of it for weeks. I was worried they'd find it. It's a nice piece … reliable."

"I've used them. They're devils to keep clean though. Is it the old make, 1915?"

"No, it's the new one. Lighter. Fits nicely in the hand. To think I was close to chucking it into the river during the week."

"How do I get hold of it then?"

"It's all at your feet in that cloth bag there. The address is there too. Just go round to them and mention the driving job. They'll be expecting you. Give the name Tom Byrne. No need to broadcast any details about yourself."

"You were pretty sure I'd take the job then?"

"I know you. You can't live off the land for the rest of your days, and I don't want you leaving the country on us."

McDaid took a last look at the river. "I'll be heading back. Those mugs won't even have missed me. I'll send a message when I want to see you again. Do you have a cigarette for your old Commandant?"

"I have a few I rolled myself."

"You're still at that malarkey? Oh well, any port in a storm." McDaid put the cigarette Holland proffered him into the inside pocket of his coat. "I'll have the pleasure of it later. Hard to light it in this wind anyway." McDaid pulled down the rim of his hat. "I'll be off then. Remember, the name's Tom Byrne."

"One minute, Commandant. Why are you giving this job to me? There're plenty of married volunteers who could do with the money."

McDaid's eyebrows tightened and he pursed his lips. "Don't look a gift horse in the mouth."

"What about Conall Caffrey? He knows Dublin better than I do. He'd be a better bodyguard."

"Caffrey's in England for the present. You're the ideal man. Forget about the others and get down to this fellow as soon as it's daylight. *Sin é*, conversation is over. Goodbye now."

McDaid turned quickly and walked rapidly away without looking back.

Holland suddenly felt a pang of loneliness. He watched McDaid's energetic retreat across O'Connell Bridge to the other side of the river. His eyes scoured the streets around him before he reached down for the cloth bag, but his fearfulness dropped away as soon as his fingers touched the hard outline of the German-made Parabellum. Its coldness was electric, like that of a living thing crackling with pent-up energy. He caught a glimpse of the gun's alien metallic sheen in the streetlight, an illusion of pure white on a surface of absolute black. Parabellums had been used in Easter 1916, the IRA shot the British with them during the War of Independence, and Irishmen died with them in their hands during the Civil War. It was heavy, weighed at least two pounds, and was much too large to fit into his coat pocket. So much for the new version, he thought.

He tucked the bag under his left arm, grasped the barrel with his right hand to stop it from slipping, and began to walk back to his digs in Stoneybatter. The heavy metallic weight of the gun filled him with a peculiar comfort. The raw smell of gun oil circulated in his head.

Having reached Church Street, he halted briefly and placed the bag on the ground in front of him while pretending to tie his shoelaces. He heard nothing but sensed the presence of someone watching him. When he started moving again, he thought he could hear another set of footsteps coming from the street behind him, footfalls calculated to match the rhythm of his own steady progress. A professional, he thought, and not a clod-hopping cop.

The faint echo of an echo that Holland was listening to was suddenly submerged by the screeching of a milk cart approaching from the top of the hill. The cart was moving slowly but the metal rims of the wheels shot an occasional spark into the air where they struck the cobblestones. After it had passed, Holland darted into Smithfield and then threw himself into the black maw of Thundercut Alley. He ran at full speed, clutching the Parabellum tightly against his chest. With high walls to the left and right of him, the unlit alleyway was so narrow that he could have easily have reached out and touched both sides. Anyone tailing him would have to be extremely foolhardy to risk following him in here, but, just in case, he halted abruptly at the bend near the Queen Street exit and crouched down to gather his breath.

The cold air was heavy with the stink of urine. In almost complete darkness Holland fumbled for the Parabellum and loaded a magazine. It clicked smoothly into position and he released the safety catch. At the far end of the alley, he heard faintly the noise of a heel slipping on the cobblestones, the sound amplified by the walls. He tensed, his finger pressed against the trigger guard. It was so dark that he was unable to see the gun in his hands. Like the blade of a knife, a shadow crossed the lighted entrance of the alley. It wavered and hovered in the air for a second and then was gone. Holland waited a few more minutes, invisible even to himself. Then he grinned, picked himself up, stashed the Parabellum in its bag and took another route home through the intimate warren of back streets and lanes behind the Smithfield Market.

2

The offices were situated in a dingy side street halfway between Dame Street and the river. When he arrived at the address, it was already late morning and the skies were darkening. The name Mundial Financing glittered amid a constellation of small silver signs at the main door of the building. Holland climbed the stairs at a lope, his body still tightly muscled and fit after an autumn's training in the mountains. On the third floor, he pushed open a door and his eyes immediately met those of a smartly dressed, dark-complexioned young woman sitting at a desk. She was click-clacking away on a typewriter in a small but impeccably equipped office.

"I'm here to see a Mr Farkas."

"Your name, please?"

"Just go tell your boss that there's a Mr Byrne here to see him."

The secretary raised her eyebrows. He was coldly perused by a pair of dark brown eyes. The examination completed, she stood up, primly smoothed out the folds of her skirt, and disappeared into a room immediately behind her desk, pointedly closing the door behind her. Holland could hear her conversing with a man inside.

Behind the allure of the secretary's perfume, he was able to detect another even more captivating aroma. It emanated from everything in the room: the expensive furniture, the waxy-headed paper in the typewriter, the bundles of Manila envelopes, the stacks of thick documents bulging from the filing cabinets. He thought: Who do these people finance? Why are they hidden away in such a dreary street when it's clear they have the where-withal for something much better? He peeped at the papers on the secretary's desk and craned his neck to take a look at the letter she was typing. All he could ascertain was that the language was not English.

"Curious, aren't we?" The secretary had returned. "Mr Farkas would like to talk to you now. I will take your coat."

"I'll keep it on, thanks."

He pushed the door open and went inside. Farkas was standing formally at his desk in a pose that Holland suspected was supposed to look military. He was about average height and fit-looking for his age, which Holland estimated to be in the mid-fifties. Despite his fair hair, his skin was sallow, as if he had once been very tanned and the colour had gradually drained away. In the large, disk-like face, the delicate nose and mouth seemed iso-lated, like features on a sketchy explorer's map. Farkas would have been a good cherub if it weren't for his eyes: Holland felt them, dark and searching, fastening onto his face.

"Tom Byrne's the name. I was told you were looking for someone to fill a position."

Farkas said something, which Holland didn't catch, and then lazily stretched out his hand. Holland extended his own hand, but Farkas, as if he had forgotten his origi-nal intention, had now changed his mind and touched him lightly on the arm instead. He looked critically at Holland's clothes.

Holland was relieved that he had kept his coat on. The suit he was wearing had once been his Sunday best, but was now worn away at the elbows and knees. His tie was stringy and out of shape and his shoes were scuffed and cracked. Farkas extracted a pince-nez from the pocket of his jacket and examined Holland even more closely.

Holland's patience was beginning to wear thin.

"You are Mr Farkas, aren't you?" he asked, stumbling over the unfamiliar-sounding name.

Farkas looked surprised.

"Ah yes, my manners, where are they? I am terribly sorry but I place great importance on first impressions. It's a habit of mine. Before conversation, one has only the magnetic personality to assess, the essence of the physical presence."

"Very interesting," Holland said. He wondered if the man was a nancy. The accent didn't help much: it was evidently based on upper-class English but was too mechanical to be convincing, as though he had to struggle with each word to keep it from being dragged down and moulded into a foreign flatness.

"Now to business. Your duties will include driving me to work and back each day…"

Holland's eyes tightened. "Wait a second. Are you telling me that I have the job? Do you not want to know anything about me?"

Farkas replaced his pince-nez, walked behind his desk and started to finger a thick portfolio.

"I know all I need to know. You have come highly recommended. And there has been a perlustration of your abilities."

"A perlustration?"

"A test."

Farkas smiled knowingly and Holland suddenly understood why he had been followed the night before.

"If anyone should ask questions, it should be you," Farkas said. "Ask all the questions you wish. You must be curious about this company? What we do and so forth."

"What your game is, you mean?"

"If you want to put it like that, yes. For example: what do you think we do?"

"I'm not well up on the world of finance, but you probably send money backwards and forwards. And I'm sure everything is done very discreetly. Otherwise, you wouldn't have chosen such a hidey-hole for an office."

Farkas beamed at him and Holland noted a white scar on his left cheek as the muscles stretched into a smile.

"Excellent. You are quite perceptive. We deal in bonds, obligations, promissory notes, stock certificates." He wagged his finger playfully. "But I do not approve of the word 'hidey-hole'. Better to say that we place a great importance on discretion, especially on our clients' behalf."

"And my wages?"

"Ah yes, let us say £4 a week to start with. Is that sufficient? You won't have to work every weekday. If you prove satisfactory, you can expect an increase after a month. And there was something about arms. Your referee said that you preferred using your own. That is perfectly in order. Just keep the weapon in the car. I have a licence for it."

Holland wondered what exactly was meant by 'using your own'.

"And I'll be driving in Ireland, not abroad?"

"Around the city for the most part. We will visit a number of clients, the embassies and consulates occasionally, merchant banks, the Stock Exchange. However, we may also have to drive farther afield; perhaps to England."

"Belfast?"

"It's not impossible. Is this a problem for you?"

"Not as long as I can stay in the car and hold the gun."

Farkas looked puzzled.

"Ah yes, the gun. You know about guns I've been told. This is very important, but of course, as with everything else, discretion is our byword. It is simply a precaution. This company deals in sensitive information, the movements of funds and so on. If we get involved in any sort of unpleasantness, it must be at the most imperceptible level."

Holland felt as if he had popped up inside a bizarre Hollywood film, with Farkas playing the role of shady continental aristocrat. His own role was still undecided. He could be the honest shamus or the mad Mick gunman, or something else entirely.

"When do you want me to start?"

"Tomorrow would be fine. There is one other matter however." Farkas' eyes traced a line from Holland's head to his shoes. He was suddenly acutely aware of the difference between himself and his new employer, who was dressed in an expensive suit, with starched collars and a silk tie fastened with a pin. "Are they the only proper clothes you have?"

Holland nodded.

"Do not concern yourself. We can have you fitted up for something suitable." Farkas reached for Holland's hand again. "I'll see you tomorrow then. If you arrive here at eight o'clock, my secretary will give you the keys to the car. It's parked at a garage in the next street: a Wolseley, four-door saloon, quite new. She'll tell you where to find it. You simply drive out to my address and I will give you instructions from there."

11

The interview was at an end. Holland left the office unsure what to think. On the street he stopped and drew cold air into his lungs. He thought about the money he would earn and the pleasure of being able to drive a car again. But the job itself sounded extraordinarily vague. Why the gun? Why did a respectable businessman need an armed chauffeur?

That night Holland drifted through the back streets on the north side of the city. He sucked thoughtfully on a cigarette and tried to ignore the stench and noise of the tenement houses, with their open hall-doors and red-raddled stairways. Carefully stopping and checking at shop-windows in case he was being followed, he gradually made his way to a well-known Republican hangout called O'Phelan's.

The bar was already full and bursting with life when he arrived. Most of the regulars were hangers on, not volunteers. Holland ignored them, although a few tried to grab his attention. He walked quietly behind the counter and knocked on a door on the other side. A panel slid back and a pair of eyes examined him unblinkingly for a couple of seconds. The door creaked open about twelve inches and Holland squeezed his way past the man on guard duty.

He entered a wood-lined room with a hatch in one wall for ordering drinks. There was a single customer only, Conall Caffrey, sitting with a glass and a pint bottle of stout: the naked light bulb hanging from the ceiling made his skin shine a waxy yellow. Caffrey jumped to his feet as soon as he caught sight of Holland. He was of medium height and heavily built with thick blond hair, flattened down with Brylcreem.

"Holland! Long time since last time! Come here. Let's be getting you a bottle of stout."

The man's accent was more refined than Holland's—South Dublin with traces of an English inflection on some words.

"I was told you'd be here. I heard you're just back from England."

"I was," said Caffrey in a hushed voice, "on a little visit. I'll tell you about it, but first we have to sit down nice and quiet like."

A bottle and glass appeared at the hatch and Caffrey passed over the money. He winked at Holland as he placed them in front of him.

"Cheapest pub in Dublin, for the likes of us at any rate."

Holland shook his head. "I've never taken to this place. No escape routes. If the Staters launch a raid, we've had it."

"You're wrong. They'll never get us in here. We bar the door, and do you see that panel there?" Caffrey pointed to a section of the wall. "It comes off and there's a passage out to the backyard. The Staters aren't clever enough to seal off the whole street. We'd be up and gone before they'd even figured out we were here."

"Yeah, and if they find out about the passage, it'd make a very handy trap. One man with a revolver could capture the lot of us."

Caffrey punched him playfully on the arm. "Always the bloody pessimist."

Holland settled back and relaxed as much as he could on the hard wooden seat. He unbuttoned his coat and hung it on the back of the chair.

"How was England?" he asked.

"I was in Ipswich for a couple of days and the amount of skirt was astonishing. I gave the girls over there the story that I was an Irish doctor seconded to the local hospital and they all fell for it. You could do with a weekend in England yourself, Holly. The English girls are amazing—pretend you're a toff and they're just asking for it, not like the Holy Mary brigade over here. A good-looking lad like yourself would have it made."

"I thought you were only supposed to dip your stick into Irish waters."

"Oh yeah, purity of the race and all that. You've been spending too much time in McDaid's company."

Holland laughed. "They'll put you away one of these days."

"Well, I'll have some fun first. Anyway, what are your plans?"

"I was thinking of heading over to Spain, but the Commandant got me a job instead."

"Not in the light-bulb company? There must be a dozen volunteers working shifts there. If we could design bulbs that blow up, we'd put the Free Staters on the run."

"No, I've got a driving job. I'm to cart this Hungarian businessman around in a fancy car. The money's all right."

Before Caffrey had a chance to reply, the door swung open and three men walked in.

They seemed surprised to see Holland. Caffrey stood up and shook their hands. "Let me introduce you to these fellas, Holly. They're just down from the Wee North. This is Jimmy and Seamus and Butty." Caffrey sat down and put his arm around Holland. "You know, I love this man. He's like a brother to me. We've had more close calls than you'd ever believe."

The Northerners looked sceptical but one of them screwed his cigarette in his mouth and offered Holland a hand. They were narrow-faced men with big muscular arms and shoulders and eyes that sparkled like cut glass in the dull light of the snug. They pushed themselves onto the bench.

One of them looked at Holland. "Have you ever been up to the occupied Six Counties yourself?" The man's eyes bored into him.

Holland felt his throat catch as he answered—a little too quickly: "No, we've never been to Belfast." He saw once again the man on the waste ground, the blood blossoming on his chest, the look of disbelief in his eyes, the recoil as the revolver bucked like a living creature in his hand. Oh yes, he and Caffrey had been to the Six Counties all right: they had run through the streets of Belfast with the harsh cries of the women behind them. They had hidden in the cellar of a safe house for two days before being shipped back to Dublin in the back of a lorry. And they had kissed the shit-laden streets of Dublin with relief when they arrived.

"I thought *you* said you were in Belfast once," continued the man turning to Caffrey. The heavily stressed vowels made Holland feel they were being interrogated.

"Ah yes," answered Caffrey, playing up the Dublin half of his own speech. "Just the once. I'd heard the women of Belfast were fine things altogether. And the rumours were true. I don't suppose any of you have a sister?" His levity was commendable, but Holland knew that all he was trying to do was cover up for Holland's gaffe.

"You'd better stay away from my sister. She wouldn't be safe with some cute Southern hoor like you."

The Northerners barked with laughter.

"The women of Belfast produce good fighting men anyway," added another. They laughed again in their peculiar, aggressive manner. "And we need them too. We're the ones done the real fighting in this country. D'ye remember '35? Up on a roof plugging mad Orangemen with the buggers in the RUC and the B Specials firing at will. That was war. And y'know, there was fuck-all in the way of help from you Southerners."

Caffrey put on his serious face. "We'll be up to help you one of these days. If we could just get de Valera off our backs."

"That's the trouble with the twenty-six counties. Each time you're getting all ready to come and help us, there's suddenly another split in the Movement and a new Chief of Staff. And now there's de Valera, the man who's able to sign his name but can't seem to read what he's signing. Ah sure he'll unite the country too—on paper. It'll all be there in black and white in his little desk drawer. I've heard we're going to have a united Ireland in his new constitution. What's it they call it now, Butty?"

"Bunreacht na hÉireann."

"What the fuck is *that* supposed to mean?" said one.

"Oh aye, it's going to make the Orangemen piss in their beds," said another.

Caffrey and Holland smiled uneasily. In an organisation full of fanatics and extremists, none were to compare with the men from the North. They were the nearest thing the Movement had to front-line troops.

The conversation meandered over the well-worn themes: the lack of new recruits, the shortage of arms and ammunition, men who had been rounded up or shot. After another drink, Caffrey and Holland made their excuses and left.

Outside, in the cold air, Caffrey punched Holland hard on the arm.

"All they asked was if *you* had been up to the North, an innocent bloody question. You look as if you've seen a ghost and start telling them that *we* have never been to

Belfast. Jesus, Holly, I'm beginning to worry that you're losing your grip." He pulled Holland closer and whispered in his ear: "Don't forget who shot a hole in their beloved hero of the Falls Road."

Holland grabbed Caffrey by the neck and yanked him close. "Yeah, Caff, and you know what bothers me: it looks like we plugged the wrong man. The Northerners got the real informer two weeks later."

Holland let go and Caffrey reeled back on his heels. His eyes were black holes in a face pale with anger. "Holland, you are out of line. We are foot soldiers, nothing else. We carry out our orders."

Holland realised he'd gone too far. "You're right. It just bothers me never getting the whole story." He clapped Caffrey on the shoulder and pretended to punch him on the arm. "You could have warned me that you were meeting a bunch of Northerners."

"I didn't know they were going to be there. Forget it. They were too drunk to notice anything. Maybe they thought your sister had been violated by some Ulsterman on the rampage."

"No sisters, no brothers."

"Yeah, I forgot. The Movement is your family."

"A shrinking family."

Caffrey caught Holland's arm and said in a plummy English accent. "Things are afoot, me lad. Don't worry about your lovely family."

"What does that mean?"

Caffrey rubbed his nose. "Bob's your uncle," he said before running off down the street.

Holland took his usual circular route through Stoneybatter back to his digs.

Back in his bedroom he could not relax enough to sleep. The Northerners had upset him. For a long time he lay in the motionless darkness trying to control the violent pictures streaming through his mind. The skin in his mouth and throat was dry, as if he had been shouting hard. Eventually he summoned the strength to pull himself out of the bed and switch on the light. There was a noggin of Jameson's whiskey in his bedside locker. He took a swig from it and walked over to the window. No other source of illumination was visible in the street: his room sailed dizzy and alone over a sea of absolute night.

3

The following morning was fresh and blustery. A clear sharp easterly had swept away the malodorous air of the previous night from the tops of the crowded tenement streets and the pigsties and cattle pens of Stoneybatter. Holland reached the Mundial office just after eight o'clock and ran into the secretary halfway up the stairs. He noticed her legs, smooth, lean and tanned. When he greeted her, she looked flustered, as though caught in some indiscretion, but quickly regained her poise and coldly handed him the keys to the car and the lock-up. When he asked for Farkas' address, she smiled coldly and gave him directions to a street in Sandymount. She told him that he did not require the house number.

Holland found the lock-up easily enough. He unhooked the padlock and swung open the heavy doors. Inside was the bulk of a Wolseley saloon. Holland had never actually sat in a luxury motorcar before, let alone driven one. He climbed inside, leant back in a seat that reeked of best-quality leather and ran his fingers along the wooden instrument panel. When he started the engine, it hummed like a colony of well-bred bees.

It took him about ten minutes to reach the Sandymount address. Farkas was standing on the street corner. To Holland's surprise his employer was wearing a crumpled mackintosh and a trilby that had seen better days. One of his long-fingered hands held a black attaché case while the other was tucked nonchalantly into his pocket. Only his sallow complexion and the continental appearance of the attaché case marked him out from the other office functionaries hurrying towards the city centre.

Holland drew in beside the kerb and shouted at him to hop in. Farkas climbed into the back seat.

"Last time I saw that look I was in school about to get a pandying from the master."

"I would like to remind you that I am your employer. We can dispense with the 'sir' but I would like a modicum of respect."

Holland caught Farkas' eyes in the mirror. "For your information I told you to hop in so as to avoid attracting attention. If I started acting the chauffeur, everyone in the street would notice, wouldn't they?"

Farkas looked at him intensely, as though his remark had made a deep impression on him.

"You are perfectly correct of course. I had no intention of insulting your intelligence."

They drove the rest of the way in silence. Farkas took out his pince-nez from an inside pocket and read through his papers while Holland concentrated on the traffic, which mostly consisted of great shoals of cyclists. Farkas thanked him when they arrived at the office and then disappeared up the stairs while Holland parked the car.

Holland had no idea what to do for the rest of the day. Back at the office the secretary ignored him. He took a seat and began to leaf through a sheaf of newspapers on a nearby table; he had never seen so many different titles before. Apart from the Irish dailies, all the British quality papers were there and at the bottom of the heap he even found old copies of *Le Figaro* (which he took to be an Italian paper) and the *Frankfurter Zeitung*.

"Does your boss get through all these every day?"

Without lifting her eyes from the document she was proofreading, the secretary said: "He reads only what he needs to know."

Pardon me for opening my gob, thought Holland. He soon grew tired of all the articles about problems in Europe, the fascists, the communists, the Spanish war (all the news seemed to be happening somewhere else these days, although it pleased him to read that the Irish fascists were still on the decline), and settled down to read the sports pages.

When he had his fill of reading the columns of black print, he watched the secretary for a while from his safe redoubt behind the newspaper. Her face had begun to fascinate him, although he did not consider her beautiful. She looked nothing like the fair-haired, rosy-cheeked girls displayed on the giant billboards beside the Phoenix Park. Her face was too long and angular, her hair a disorderly mass of black curls. But there was something about those coal black eyes, the way they were slightly slanted, as though constantly enquiring after some item she had lost. And then there was the mouth, the full red lips, even more striking because of her dark complexion, quite unlike the anaemic or painted lips of Irish girls. He wondered vaguely if she was French; her accent was difficult to place.

Lunchtime arrived but nothing was said. The secretary took out a packet of sandwiches from her bag and began to eat. She devoured her food in short predatory bites.

Holland left the office without saying a word and found a place selling hot meals for a reasonable price on Dame Street. He treated himself to the mixed grill, "the whole show" as the man said—sausages, egg, liver and fried potatoes for two shillings—and washed it down with tea. Then he returned to the office, collected some newspapers and sat in the car to read them until Farkas emerged about two hours later. Again they drove in silence; the only sound, besides the changing of gears, was the occasional ruffle of papers from the backseat. Holland dropped him off at the same street corner in Sandymount. Farkas alighted on the pavement and glanced back at Holland.

"That suit you're wearing; it really is the only one you have?"

Holland nodded.

"Well, we'll have to find you something more suitable tomorrow. And a hat of course."

"Whatever you say, boss," said Holland and drove off. He took the coast road for the pleasure of it, stopped the car beside the beach and opened the window. The cold, antiseptic air filled his lungs and this sensation made him recall his mother's face. She was young again, just as she was in the old photographs he had of her, smiling as the wind tugged at her hair. She does not see him: she exists in the moment, perhaps before he was born, when her life was happy. He restarted the car, conscious of a weakness inside him, a fatal vulnerability that even membership of the Movement cannot heal.

He drove to the city centre, returned the Wolseley to the lock-up and walked to his digs.

Mrs Mullen had a meal waiting for him when he arrived.

"How was your first day?"

"I sat and read newspapers all day in front of a snobby-looking secretary. She could hardly be bothered looking up when I asked her a question."

"Do you miss not having a girlfriend?"

Holland thought for a few seconds. "I was doing a steady line for a while, but in my business that's not always easy. It didn't work out."

Mrs Mullen placed her hand on his shoulder and squeezed it. "You're a good man. You'll make some girl very happy. Can I get you more potatoes?"

"Yes, thanks. By the way, if anyone rings up asking for a Tom Byrne, it'll really be me they're wanting." Mrs Mullen gave him a questioning look. "It's because of the Special Branch. If they know I have a job, they'll try to get me kicked out of it."

She nodded.

"My own husband will be out in less than a month. I know how hard things will be for him."

"You must be looking forward to having him back?"

"Oh, yes indeed—of course I am."

That was the night Mrs Mullen visited him in his room. Afterwards he could not really convince himself that her visit had come as a surprise. Since his arrival, she had paid an unusual amount of attention to him, as though he were a special guest rather than an ordinary tenant. She was constantly brushing his coat or asking his advice or wondering whether he might be hungry or thirsty.

She came into his room just before dawn. The squeaking of the doorknob woke him immediately. She was dressed only in her shift, her large breasts protruding through the thin fabric. Holland was at first unsure whether or not he was dreaming. Mrs Mullen held her finger to her lips as she climbed into the bed beside him. The springs creaked in protest. Her body filled up the bed with raw animal warmth.

"Go on, touch them," she said.

He ran his fingers inside her nightdress and up her sides and felt the weight of her breasts, their coolness contrasting with the intense warmth of her belly.

She began to feel between his legs.

"Mrs Mullen, this is not right: we can't. What about your husband?"

"I think you can," she said.

He inserted himself into her. The bed lurched and bucked, screeching mechanically in time with the phases of their passion. He gently stroked her clitoris with his trigger finger as his penis slid in and out. He slowed down and rested, explored her wetness for a while before continuing. Mrs Mullen moaned like a young girl; her eyes rolled as though he had injected her with some drug. His own desire grew steadily until he felt he could no longer hold back. Mrs Mullen, sensing it, grasped his buttocks and pulled him even further into her. And he came, in long waves of pleasure, and then floundered, shaken by the recoil, clutching at her large prone body, her breasts, her face; unable for some reason to look her in the eye.

When he had caught his breath again, she kissed him quickly on the forehead and patted his hair. "By the way, you can call me Velma. But remember, never in front of the other tenants."

At the Mundial office, Holland's day again consisted of ferrying Farkas to work and then waiting in the car or the front office. For something to do, he occupied a tiny side room to the office where there was a table and chair and a couple of filing cabinets. With some tools he had taken from his digs, he disassembled the Parabellum pistol, cleaned and examined each part, applied oil, and checked the magazine and loading mechanism. This took him about two hours. When he was satisfied that it was in working order, he began to reassemble it. He had just started when the secretary arrived with a cup of coffee.

He looked up without any sign of friendliness as she placed the cup on the table.

"Thanks, but I usually drink tea," he said dryly.

She seemed unfazed; her eyes registered no slight. "Mr Farkas asked me to come with it. It's the best Brazilian coffee."

She looked as if she was about to turn and leave again, but something about the gun made her stay.

"It's a Pistole Parabellum, yes?"

"I've only heard them called Parabellums, but you're right." Holland was conscious of her body, her thigh pressed against the table. With her strange features and immobile eyes, she reminded him of a statue. Only the faint motion of her chest indicated that she was a living woman.

"My father had one once, when he was an officer. On the Galician Front."

"So you *are* a German?" he asked eagerly, suddenly desperate for her to continue to talk to him.

There was a fleeting smile; her eyes flashed him a look filled with irony. He had made some kind of error, but couldn't guess what it was. His face coloured and he again concentrated his attention on the gun. The ejector, the trigger bar plunger, lay directly in front of his fingers. But he couldn't remember what to do next.

Without looking at him, the secretary pushed the cup in front of him, saying "Enjoy your coffee," then turned around and moved towards the door.

But he was hungry for company, tired of his own trackless thoughts.

"Wait a second, please. I'll show you something."

She stopped, as if surprised by her own interest, and he continued. "You see all these parts here. There are nearly thirty of them, and I haven't even fully taken it apart. The Parabellum is the most complicated automatic pistol around. I want you to test me. I'll close my eyes; you pick up a part and put it in my hand and I'll tell you what it is."

"A game, is that it?" She turned her head away from him. "I'm not sure I have the time."

"It'll only take a second. Go on."

She hesitated, looked at him again; the eyes suddenly softened.

"All right."

Holland covered his eyes and the secretary placed one of the parts in his hand.

"It's the coupling link for the recoil spring."

The secretary was unimpressed. "How do I know you're telling the truth?"

Holland pointed to a greasy manual listing the parts. She checked his answer.

"How impressive," she said smiling. Her teeth were very white, cushioned between plump red lips.

"Try again."

She placed a new part in his hand.

"The trigger bar pin."

"That's not what is here. I'm sorry."

"It's also called the sear pin."

"That's correct. I have another one here you will not guess."

"Try me."

Holland's mind went back and forth visualizing every aspect of the Parabellum in three dimensions but the part escaped him. Not only could he not identify it, he could not even work out where it belonged. After a few moments agonising, he gave up and opened his eyes.

"What the hell is this? This has nothing to do with the Parabellum."

"No, it's the top of my fountain pen."

Again her perfect white teeth gleamed through a pert smile. She turned and left the room.

After her departure, her perfume remained floating in the air like the scent of an exotic plant. Holland returned to the delicate task of reassembling the pistol.

At lunchtime, Farkas announced that Holland was to go with him to find a suit.

"Don't worry, the company will pay the bill. Come on; get ready. You do not need that coat."

"I do need it," said Holland. He slipped the Parabellum into the bag before following his employer out of the office.

They visited half-a-dozen tailors' shops in the city centre but although Farkas carefully appraised Holland in each of the suits he tried on, nothing pleased him. They ended up buying an off-the-peg suit in a gentlemen's outfitters on Grafton Street. Farkas was not too happy about the width of the trousers—he told Holland that closer-fitting trousers were in style on the Continent—but the cut and material were of good quality. The price, £11.10, shocked Holland, but Farkas assured him that this was perfectly in order.

They then looked at shoes. The tailor tried to persuade Holland to try out a contraption that used x-rays to measure customers' feet but he declined. They found ready-made shoes that fitted. Farkas purchased two pairs. Holland felt uncomfortable about having things bought for him but his employer was adamant.

"It is important for the firm that you look your best," he told him.

The tailor chalked in the places where the suit was to be taken in, and Holland arranged to pick it up the following week.

Late that night, Mrs Mullen, or Velma as she now insisted he called her, visited him again. She wore the same diaphanous nightdress, and the bed creaked as noisily as before when she clambered on top of him. This time he whispered in her ear that they should take precautions.

"No need. I can't have children anyway. Just lie back and enjoy yourself."

He took her at her word.

The week went by, reading newspapers, driving the car and exchanging a few pleasantries with the secretary. At the end of it, he summed up the result. He had found a well-paid job that involved no real work, a woman who required no commitment, an important role in the Movement but without any risk. He knew he ought to be happy and grateful for all this good fortune, but he wasn't; all he felt was a gnawing sense of unease.

He spent the weekend drinking with Caffrey and some other comrades.

"McDaid, our king of the leprechauns, he'll be wanting to see you again soon," Caffrey told him. He ran a finger down his nose. "The big plan; it's all to do with the big plan. Have patience. You'll see."

Holland believed him and ordered, with his first week's wages, another round for his friends.

4

On the following Monday, Holland picked up his new suit from the outfitter's and wore it to work. Farkas looked at him approvingly when he arrived at the office. He cuffed Holland's arms and felt the material between his fingers and thumb. "Excellent work. Good room in the shoulders. We shall order another, so you always have one in reserve."

"Yes," said Holland, "bloodstains are a devil to get out."

"Good," said Farkas humorously, although his smile was automatic. "Tomorrow morning I would like you to drive out to the mail boat in Dun Laoghaire and pick up some clients. You're to take good care of them, my friend. They're our lifeblood. Sabine will accompany you."

It was the first time Holland had heard Farkas use the secretary's first name. The three syllables struck him as cold, hard and precise. It sounded more like the name of a precious stone than of a human being.

When they arrived at the office the next day, Farkas sent the secretary down to Holland who remained in the Wolseley. Sabine carefully installed herself in the back-seat.

Holland watched her in the rear-view mirror as he negotiated the traffic. On a straight stretch he began to fiddle with a cigarette and a box of matches.

"Mr Byrne, I'd prefer it if you didn't smoke in the car. I can't do anything about the clients, but when we're alone, please."

"Right oh," said Holland. He stowed the box of matches and cigarette in his pocket. "So you've met these characters from England before?"

"No, I have never seen them before."

"How are we going to recognise them? Will they all be standing in a row wearing red carnations?"

Sabine did not find his comment amusing. "I'll know who they are."

"We could have picked them up at Amiens Street Station. It would have been easier."

"Just concentrate on the driving, please."

Her final 'please' put a bullet in the conversation. Holland decided to keep his mouth shut after that.

As they drove along the coast road, the sea, expansive and shimmering under the spring sun, opened up the horizon but there was no indication that Sabine noticed it.

Suddenly the long wooden mass of the customs building came into view and Holland sneaked in behind a taxi and parked. He hopped out to open the door for Sabine.

She spotted the clients almost as soon as she had stepped out of the car. There were three of them: two short men in their forties, and one who was taller than Holland and younger than the other two. Their clothes were impeccably tailored, the folds razor sharp, their dark hair immaculately cut and slicked back. They reminded Holland of characters in a gangster film.

"Are they Italians?"

"No," Sabine said severely.

She smoothed down her dress and went over to meet them.

Holland stood by the door and waited. The tall man walked directly up to the car and without saying a word thrust a large suitcase towards him. Holland made no movement to take it. The man looked at him, his eyes questioning. Despite his obvious strength, he could not have held it in that position for more than another couple of seconds. Sabine caught Holland's eye and nodded; he swallowed his pride and took the case.

"You had a pleasant crossing?" Sabine asked the two smaller men.

They said something to her in a guttural language Holland did not recognise. Sabine smiled and replied, hesitantly, in the same language. The men laughed together. Their teeth seemed very white, interspersed with flashes of gold.

"It's a bit parky here, my friend," one of the small men said to Holland. Holland smiled without understanding what the man had meant. "My name's Greene by the way, and this is my associate, Mr Slade." Mr Slade bobbed his head. The large man, clearly a bodyguard, was not introduced. Holland put their suitcase in the boot. The clients, clutching their briefcases as tightly as they could, positioned themselves carefully in the back of the car. They talked in a mixture of English and their own language as they made themselves comfortable. Holland opened the door and Sabine placed herself in the passenger seat beside him. He could not help noticing the slimness of her legs and her perfume as it mixed with the masculine odour of the men's aftershave and the leather upholstery of the car.

Holland turned the Wolseley around and drove back to the city centre.

5

Six a.m., a crowded pub close to the Smithfield Market, filled with cigarette and pipe smoke and the warm fug of cow dung and stale clothes. Outside it was still pitch black: carts and lorries rumbled along the cobble-stoned streets, but their progress was everywhere curtailed. Cattle, cruelly urged on by men with spiked ash sticks, or cajoled by kinder souls with caresses or rubs, clogged every thoroughfare leading to the market, their smell and noise overpowering. Most had been unloaded from the Cabra yard on the Great Southern and Western line or from Liffey Junction on the Great Western Midland line, and were now being driven to the vast system of pens that divided up the market. Here and there, a goat could be seen, its head nervously bobbing between the great brown sides of the beasts; brought with the herd to pacify them, and for good luck.

Holland and McDaid were sitting at a table in a corner of the pub surrounded by cattle-dealers and drovers. A collie, its canines removed, snaked through the thick jungle of legs, occasionally stopping to lap up beer from the floor.

Holland yawned uncontrollably. He had just given his Commandant a brief account of the visitors from England.

"Here we are again at the crack of dawn. Why can't we meet at normal times?"

"The early bird," said McDaid winking. "You should consider it a privilege. This place is strictly reserved for the cattlemen. It's only because I know the owner that we're allowed in."

Holland took a sip from his glass. "What in sweet Jaysus' name is this?"

"Have you never tried it before? That's coffee mixed with whiskey and a bit of treacle to sweeten it. The drovers swear by it. If they drink that, they never get a cold, no matter what the weather."

"So the detectives aren't watching you any more?"

"They're taking a break from it. Oh yes; tell Mrs Mullen when you see her that her husband was asking for her. He hopes to be released before Christmas. No mail is getting in or out: some of them are talking about a hunger strike."

Holland opened his eyes wide. "Christmas! I thought he'd be out in a few weeks. What's he in for anyway?"

"He was caught at a safe house, tricking around with the private parts of a Browning automatic."

Holland began to enjoy the bitter drink. His body radiated warmth.

"You know it was a whorehouse you picked him up at, that Belfast man," McDaid continued. "The women, you see; that was his weakness. Ironic really."

"Why ironic?"

McDaid smiled. "Shot dead by a man who has given up on the women."

"I haven't given them up."

McDaid smiled archly and clapped the table. He examined intently a group of dealers, easily distinguishable from the drovers by their wide-brimmed hats and double coats. The men were complaining bitterly about the recent closure of Liffey Junction to passengers, which

33

meant that they had to take a different train to Amiens Station on the other side of the city.

"Is there anything else?" Holland asked.

"I have something important to impart to you. But first I have a wee present."

He handed Holland a long official document. "It's in your new name and it's genuine. You can use it as ID anywhere at all."

Holland took the driving licence and unfolded it.

"You have to put your signature on it, of course. Do that as soon as you get home."

"Thanks. What was it you wanted to tell me?"

McDaid looked around before speaking. Holland waited patiently. Burly men holding glasses of beer or hot whiskies shuffled in disorderly orbits around them. McDaid's head craned forward. "I heard you've a talent for languages. You picked up the Irish in no time at all."

"It gave me something to do in jail, besides hatching escape plans. What about it?"

"Ó Cadhain told me once that the German and the Irish were very similar. Grammatically speaking that is. Master the one and you can easily master the other, he used to say."

McDaid downed the remains of his drink and placed the glass deliberately back on the table.

"Are you asking me to learn German to spy on my employer?"

McDaid regarded him with the look of a teacher surprised by a pupil's clever remark.

"Something like that. Try catching some of the conversation between this Farkas fella and his visitors."

"How am I supposed to learn this language? By reading their minds?"

"Oh you're the grouchy one first thing in the morning! I have some books here, under the table. Take them with you when you leave. I'd be interested to find out what all these foreign jackos are jawing about. Make a list of where they go and what they do as well."

"Maybe I should take notes in Irish," Holland said sarcastically.

"That's the spirit. *Sinn é*. I have to be off now."

McDaid disappeared like a wraith into the thick forest of coats. Holland felt under the table for the books and remained for a few minutes more before leaving. He then dodged through a herd of calves timidly making their way down the street, brushed past a tiny nun collecting money for charity, and dived into the warren of laneways that lay behind all the main thoroughfares of Dublin's city centre, the dark communal world of the poor and the revolutionary.

The visitors remained for three days, staying at the Castle Hotel on Gardiner's Row. Holland took them everywhere. Farkas refused to allow them to as much as place their feet on a pavement unless it was to step into or out of the Wolseley. On the first day they motored to Celbridge, and had lunch in an expensive restaurant. Sabine remained at the office while Holland was provided with sandwiches. Farkas seemed to be intent on keeping Holland in his place but he had not reckoned on his visitors' curiosity about the country they were visiting.

The next day, the bodyguard was left behind and Holland took them for a drive in the Wicklow Mountains. Sabine sat in the front passenger seat. After they had been driving for an hour, Mr Greene said: "I never knew that Ireland was such a beautiful country. Look at these mountains, these lakes! We have nothing like this anywhere near London. There must be stories too; you can't have a landscape like this without good stories, can you? All these ruins—are there stories to go with them?"

Sabine and Farkas exchanged glances. Neither of them knew anything about the countryside they were driving through. Sabine wasn't even sure whether they were north or south of the city. Egged on by Mr Greene's enthusiasm, Farkas gave Holland a questioning look. With nothing better to do, Holland began to give them a running commentary.

He was not much good at telling stories but he was well able to describe where they were going and what tales were connected to each place, and he knew the Wicklow Mountains well since he had done most of his weapon training there. Holland's main problem was not to reveal too much. His reticence tended to increase the interest of his listeners and his mind worked furiously to entertain them when he realised that they were passing woodlands that concealed an arms dump or a shooting range.

Farkas asked Holland to suggest a scenic route before they descended to Dublin. Holland took them past Blessington and through the Wicklow Gap as far as Glendalough. Since the weather was fine, he stopped the car and suggested that they have a look at the monastery. For once, Farkas agreed to allow his visitors roam free.

They clambered over a stile and walked along a gravel path. The air was eerily still. Blue mountains rose up like walls enclosing the narrow valley. When they had walked through the trees, the shapes of the ancient stone build-ings and the round tower appeared before them like a tableau.

"It's like Shangri-la!" Mr Greene exclaimed.

"Perhaps we should have some tea here before we return to Dublin," Farkas said.

He had noticed a sign advertising a tearoom. They went inside: the owner, a stout middle-aged woman with red cheeks, ran out to meet them. She was very pleased to be able to welcome English visitors, who were, she told them, "so rare these days". The tearoom was decorated in the Victorian style still popular in such places. They sat at a table covered with a white linen tablecloth and Farkas ordered pots of tea and scones.

Mr Greene insisted that Holland sit beside him. He laid his hand on Holland's wrist, as though Holland was a favourite nephew: "Tell me, young man, what did you do before you started chauffeuring?"

Holland cast a glance at Farkas before replying: "I worked with cars."

"Have you had much schooling?"

"Christian Brothers." He was suddenly aware that none of those present would have heard of the Christian Brothers but went on lamely. "There wasn't money enough ... to continue."

"And your parents? Your father; what does he do, may I ask?"

"He's dead. He died in 1918."

"In the war?"

"No, the Spanish flu."

"And your mother?"

"My mother died two years ago."

"I'm sorry to hear that. But you're managing well; you have prospects. I'm sure you'll have a bright future." With those words he patted Holland's hand again and smiled sadly out of the window.

It was at this point that Holland caught Sabine stealing a glance in his direction. Before she turned away, he thought he noticed some hint of warmth in those dark brown eyes, and a feeling of hope blazed momentarily inside him. It seemed to him that for the first time she had begun to regard him as a fellow human being, and not just as a desperado with a gun.

Whatever the deal was, it was concluded the following day. On the final evening Farkas emerged from his office and went out to see Holland, who was working on the car. He passed an envelope into his hand.

"This is for all the extra work," he said. Before he walked away, he rubbed his cheek and looked at Holland. "There's one other thing. I want to take our guests out tonight. Would you like to keep us company?"

Holland shrugged and smiled.

"Good. You can pick us up at the hotel about eight o'clock."

When he had gone, Holland turned his attention to the envelope. There was no name on it and no message inside it but it did contain two brand new £5 notes.

6

That evening, Holland waited in the Wolseley outside the Castle Hotel. The only semblance of life on the street was a paper wrapper dancing on the pavement with delicate unexpected pirouettes. All the same he unfastened the glove compartment and caressed the rounded butt of the Parabellum.

Suddenly Farkas burst out of the hotel arm in arm with Mr Greene, both men smiling and laughing, the other two men in tow. Holland remained at the wheel while the passengers organised themselves. Farkas sat in the front seat while the guests occupied the back, the bodyguard blocking most of Holland's view through the rear windows. Everyone appeared to be happy, as though, against the odds, they had all managed to make a killing at the same game of cards.

Mr Greene clapped both Holland and Farkas on the back and kept his hands fastened there, as if loathe to lose physical contact with them.

"Where are we going, my friends?" he asked.

Farkas opened the window. "There's a jazz quartet playing in the Shelbourne. I've booked a table."

Then he said something rapidly in another language. Three of the words—*in der Nähe*—suddenly leapt to life in Holland's head; he knew he had read them in one of the books McDaid had given him. So this was German then, he thought; understandable, intelligible, unlike the strange dialect Sabine used when she spoke to the guests.

Farkas made a nod to Holland who started the engine.

It took them only a few minutes to reach St Stephen's Green. Besides the usual cyclists and a few horse-drawn cabs, the traffic was light.

"Not exactly the West End, is it?" joked the bodyguard.

Mr Greene coughed. "It's so relaxing here after London. Does a person good. Friendly atmosphere, nice people, not all the hurly-burly."

Holland positioned the car where it would be easy to get away fast.

The men clambered out, the bodyguard bringing up the rear, his head swivelling automatically to scan to the side and behind them, rather than looking to the front. Holland was impressed with this artful repression of natural instinct.

Before getting out, Farkas turned to Holland and handed him a note. "You will find Sabine at this address. She'll be expecting you."

Even though he knew nothing salacious was meant, Holland felt a sliver of excitement run through him: the untouchable Sabine, the doe-eyed Sabine, was somewhere waiting for *him*.

He found the street where she lived without much difficulty. It was one of the many decaying Georgian terraces behind the Rathmines Road. Compared to the rest of the city, the area was still quite respectable, but even here Holland had difficulty reading the numbers in the dim gaslight of the street and had to get out and walk before he found the right house. Sabine's flat was in a basement, its doorway gloomily overshadowed by the massive brick steps leading to the main entrance. He rang the bell, his fingertip unusually conscious of the smoothness of the button. After a few seconds he rang again, but the flat remained in darkness. He rapped the door with his knuckles. Again nothing. He stood there in the dark, uncertain what to do, when a voice called to him from above. The words were tremulous and unreal, as though from the voiceover in a film. He looked up and caught sight of a middle-aged woman.

"Young man," she called. "Sabine is up here with me. Please come." He went up the steps and she beckoned him inside. "I asked Sabine to have a look at some of my things."

Her accent was not just Anglo-Irish; he was listening to the voice of the old Ascendancy. As McDaid would have said, there was the smell of money gone about her. Holland wondered if she had been burnt out of some big house by the IRA, perhaps by someone he knew.

Meekly he followed her inside. The hall smelled of candles, expensive scent and musty carpets. He could see Sabine in one of the rooms leading off the hall. She was standing on a chair wearing a long backless black dress, which accentuated her narrow waist and her skin colour, giving her, in Holland's eyes at least, the aura of a movie star. Her fingers were teasing a long pearl necklace, the sort that had been popular a decade earlier. The necklace accentuated the shape of her small, round breasts. She was suddenly aware that he was looking at her, and he became conscious that he was staring. They looked blankly at each other without uttering a word until the Anglo-Irish lady broke in and asked to be introduced.

"This is Mrs Fitzgibbons, my landlady. And this is Byrne. I don't know his first name."

Mrs Fitzgibbons shook his hand. "I think Sabine mentioned you to me."

"No, I did not," Sabine said abruptly.

Holland gazed up at her: "Farkas asked me to take you to the club."

"Yes, I know. Is that really the only suit you have?"

Holland was wearing one of the two suits Farkas had bought for him.

"Really, Sabine, what a way to talk to the young man!" Mrs Fitzgibbons pretended to be shocked but seemed to be enjoying the situation. Holland, in any case, wasn't offended. He was a little surprised by the intimate terms between tenant and landlady, but then again his own circumstances were hardly conventional.

"The car's parked outside," he said.

Sabine smiled: "I didn't think you had it in your pocket."

Mrs Fitzgibbons began to fluster with a needle and thread. "We'll be finished in a minute, young man. I'm just mending the hem of her gown. Women's things, you understand."

Holland reddened, mumbled something about waiting for her outside and left. He walked back to the car and drove it to the door. Then he got out and stood waiting on the empty street. To pass the time he lit a cigarette, one he had prepared earlier, shielding the orange tip from the rain that had now begun to fall in fine silver threads.

Sabine came out before he had finished smoking, moving with surprising litheness in the long dress. She barely glanced at him, relegating him, he felt, to the status of an attending servant. She was wearing a coat fringed with a deep fur collar and a small Robin Hood cap. Holland opened the door of the passenger seat; he did not want her to sit in the back and treat him like a taxi driver. She sat in smoothly without saying anything, and adjusted her clothes. He jabbed at the self-starter and reversed the car to turn. In a few seconds they were motoring to the city centre. He wanted badly to show off, but the engine seemed sluggish and noisy, each movement

he made exaggerated as though the Wolseley was suddenly demanding a greater effort from him. Sabine did
not seem impressed.

"Have you been to the Shelbourne before?" he asked
by way of conversation as they passed Rathmines Town
Hall.

Sabine deigned to glance at him. Her eyes seemed liq-
uid, light igniting in them from the faintly luminous glow
of the dashboard.

"Yes," she said.

Sabine's mind was elsewhere. The strangeness of her
circumstances disturbed her. All that had previously been
familiar to her—her home, her family, and her country—
were now so far away and long ago that only the most
universal phenomena gave her comfort. There was the
night, there was the rain, making delicate patterns against
the glass, there were the clothes containing her and a tight
feeling behind her forehead because she was tired. This
was all she had left. Everything else had been taken from
her. She became aware that Holland was talking.

"Pardon me?" she said.

"I suppose it must be lonely. In a strange city, far from
your family."

She was momentarily surprised that he had read her
mood.

"Yes, sometimes," she answered with some feeling.

Holland felt emboldened. "Maybe you need to get out
a bit," he said turning his head. Sabine stared at the passing
buildings and said nothing. Holland continued, his breath
short: "We could maybe go and see a film or do something
one evening."

"You want to go out with me? Is that what you're
asking?"

"Yes, I suppose."

"What do they give you to do this job? £4 a week to carry a gun and risk your life? That means your life in a year is worth £208, less than the price of a second-hand car."

"I'll take that as a no."

Sabine looked across at him. "I'm not one of your shop girls."

Holland parked close to the club and walked Sabine to the entrance. The doorman gave him a darting look as though to tell him that he knew he was simply a hired hand like himself, but ushered them in just the same. The place was crowded, voluminous smoke shrouding the largest and noisiest groups. He mentioned Farkas' name to a waiter and they were shown to his table.

Farkas eyed them hungrily as they approached, as though they had arrived to save him. He made elaborate gestures to introduce them to their seats. Mr Greene was smoking a cigar and just finishing what sounded like a long and complicated joke. Both the bodyguard and Slade laughed uproariously, but Farkas could barely muster a smile.

The deal has been done, thought Holland, and the man is exhausted.

Sabine was now suddenly the centre of attention: the men admired her clothes and hair. A look passed between her and Farkas so fleeting that Holland barely caught it. He felt momentarily disgusted. He had the impression that he had witnessed a message between a pimp and his whore.

After their drinks were served, Farkas asked Holland to pick up the linen cloth he used to clean his pince-nez from the glove compartment of the car. When he got outside, Holland noticed that there were half-a-dozen more vehicles parked by the kerb. One of them, a blue Packard, looked suspicious. The inside of the car was in darkness but he spotted the glow of a cigarette from the passenger seat, burning like a tiny sun.

7

It was a Saturday—late afternoon. Holland was returning to the city centre after a visit to a garage in Rathgar to have the gears of the Wolseley checked. It was his fifth week in the job and he had fallen into an easy routine. His only concern at the moment was the lack of information coming from the Movement. Caffrey continued to be unusually cagey and there was little indication that a new campaign was being prepared.

Holland was swinging right at the foot of Rathgar Road when his eye was mesmerised by a sight so strange that he almost lost control of the car. He pulled into the kerb on the opposite side to get a better look. Across from him, Sabine was defacing a poster, wrenching it piece by piece from a wall. Surrounding her were at least fifteen onlookers, some of whom were vigorously remonstrating with her. As he watched, one of them, a large young man, grabbed her by the arm to restrain her, but she continued to shred the poster with her free hand. Holland knew that it wouldn't be long before a policeman plodded into view and took her into custody.

He was momentarily at a loss. Strictly speaking he was not supposed to intervene; he couldn't risk a run-in with the Gardaí, and there were so many people present that a getaway would be difficult. The change in Sabine had also confused him. At first he couldn't believe it was she. All her self-control seemed to have disappeared. There was rage and frustration in her eyes. Her hair had loosened itself from the grips that normally kept it in check and tresses cascaded like an ebony waterfall over her face.

Holland's fingers drummed rhythmically on the steering wheel. His eyes skirted the street and the junction as far he could see in either direction, up and down Rathmines Road. Sabine was now being restrained by a woman as well as by the beefy young man, who looked suspiciously like a Blueshirt.

Holland drove off, turned right at the junction and parked the car in a laneway. He then walked as unhurriedly as he could back to where Sabine was trapped. He could hear her raised voice even before he saw her. She was screaming at them, calling them all fascists and Nazis. She was probably right about some of them, thought Holland. While crossing the road, he noticed an unmistakable flash of illegal blue serge under the beefy thug's jacket.

Holland cut a path through the crowd. They parted for him as if a higher authority had sent him. The new suit and his height helped. He could suddenly see the young Blueshirt at close quarters: hands like pink sausages were grasping Sabine's coat. Holland resisted the temptation to walk over immediately and plant his fist into the middle of his face.

Instead, like an actor announcing a sudden change of plot in a play, he shouted: "I think this should be dealt with by the proper authority." The words struck home, their effect on the crowd like a sudden shower of rain.

He grasped Sabine's arm and disentangled her from the thug in the blue shirt. She followed him meekly, her anger dissipated. But the mob had not finished with them.

A woman shrieked: "This was a perfectly legal meeting. She'll have to pay for them posters." The Blueshirt caught up with them and put his face up to Holland's, close enough for him to see cloudy streaks in the grey irises. Holland decided to react. He'd noticed a tram approaching on the other side of Rathmines Road. He grabbed the Blueshirt's hand and twisted it back. The man dropped to his knees and Holland finished him off with a short, hard punch to the jaw. His movements were so fast that most of the people behind them were not aware of what he had done.

They started to run. No one came after them. They crossed the road. Holland took Sabine's hand as the tram doors opened; her fingers were like ice. The conductor was too busy peering at the spectacle on the other side of the street to notice them climb aboard and take a seat. They were both out of breath. With a lurch, the tram accelerated away from the angry mob, the posters and the young fascist rolling on the ground.

"Do you have the price of the fare?" asked Holland innocently. "All I have is a pound note."

"Yes, yes." She collected herself, breathed in slowly. "I do have some money. Where are we going exactly?"

Holland laughed. Where should he take Sabine?

"We're heading towards my part of town. This tram will drop us off at Nelson's Pillar if you're interested in going that far."

"You know, I thought you were some kind of local gangster … when you started."

"Well, I'm not. Whatever I am, I'm not a gangster."

"I don't really care now. I'm just glad you're on our side. I'm sorry, I know it was a foolish thing to do but I could simply not stand to go past those posters. They were for a meeting to support the fascists in Spain.

Don't people here understand anything? It will be like Germany."

"Some of my friends are fighting for the Republic in Spain."

Sabine touched his sleeve, as if to acknowledge his new status in her life.

Holland would have been quite happy for the tram ride to continue for hours. He had Sabine so close to him, her scent enclosing them, as the city passed by in a harsh staccato of grey buildings.

"How did you end up in Ireland?" he asked softly.

"I have some relations in London. I went there from Germany to improve my English. Then I heard about this job with Farkas and I decided to take it." She shifted her body slightly away from his and started to put her hair into some kind of order. Holland felt slightly embarrassed. He sensed the eyes of the other passengers. "I didn't know anything about this country until I came," Sabine continued. "I saw a film when I was in London. A new film but it was from the time the British were here. What was the name of that film? Something with the word 'enemy'. There was a tall, blond man in it. He led the Irish." She smiled. "He looked a bit like something from a Nazi poster actually. In any case, he fell in love with the daughter of the English governor here. It was the usual kind of romantic plot. She betrayed him, I think. Do you know this film?"

Holland shook his head.

"It didn't prepare me for Ireland. It was more Hollywood. This country is very different from what I imagined."

"It had a happy ending then, the film?"

"In a way. The daughter of the English leader helped the Irish and the English to make peace. But some of the Irish rebels wanted to keep fighting—I don't know why—and they planned to kill the tall, blond man. She tried to stop them but they did it anyway: his best friend was the one who aimed the gun at him when he was making a speech. But the blond man survived somehow and the couple kissed at the end."

"Maybe I *have* seen that film," said Holland. He felt a sudden craving for tobacco.

They were silent for a few moments until Sabine noticed something on the side of his face.

"That scar. Did you get it in a fight?"

"Yes," said Holland, feeling the line of his jaw. "There used to be a crowd on the North Side called the Animal Gang. They called themselves fascists but most of them were just criminals. A Republican friend of mine exchanged words with them on the street: he probably provoked them, knowing him, and I helped him to get away before they killed him. And now I have this as a souvenir."

"So you saved his life, just like you saved me?"

Holland could not tell whether Sabine's smile was sarcastic or genuine.

"The Animal Gang were a lot more dangerous than the big countryman who was after you. The one who gave me this had a cutthroat razor. Thank God he didn't make his swipe a bit lower down or I wouldn't be here talking to you."

Sabine closed her eyes and smiled. "You Irish are so fatalistic. Whatever happens, it is always God this and that, and he must be thanked. No matter how bad it is, 'it could always be worse'. And when it's good, it's 'not too bad'."

Holland laughed. "You're beginning to pick up an Irish accent. They'll start taking you for a native if you're not careful."

Sabine was suddenly serious. "I don't think so. Everyone asks me if I am from Italy or Spain. And when I say I come from Germany, they look down at their boots and say 'aha'."

"I wouldn't worry too much about people here. There's a lot of ignorance. They know nothing about the outside world. Most of them haven't travelled."

"Have you?"

Holland smiled. "I'm ignorant too. I've never been abroad, unless you want to count a trip to the Six Counties."

He felt foolish as soon as he said it. There was no need to mention the North. Her physical closeness drew words out of him like a magnet. He fought the desire to tell her everything about himself, about his role in the Movement, about the person he really was.

They got off the tram at Nelson's Pillar in O'Connell Street. Sabine said that she had to get home. Holland said he would accompany her. Sabine shook her head as though she was saying no but tilting it slightly in the same move-ment; a question mark in a negative sentence. Holland waited. He could see her thinking, and he had time to wait. She was remembering the fanatics gathered at Rathmines.

"Would it be too much trouble if… ?"

"If I went back with you? Not at all, I have to go that way to pick up the car. We can get the No. 22 from Aston Quay."

"Yes."

"But I wouldn't advise you to head back yet."

To their left, a tram disgorged its occupants; the peo-ple flowed around and between them in a thick current of coats and hats. Holland could not make out what Sabine was saying. She looked so slim and fragile, as though she were about to be swept away.

He caught her arm and pulled her closer to him.

Her mouth beside his ear, she said: "So you're the expert on mobs and thugs."

It wasn't what he had expected her to say. He didn't like her sarcasm.

"We'll go back in an hour. There'll be no trouble then."

The crowd suddenly dispersed. He moved her quickly away, away from the trams, over to the pavement. A man with a box camera wanted to take their picture. Holland blocked the lens with his hand and told him to leave them alone.

The man whinged: "It's only a shilling."

They hurried past, Holland flushed and perspiring. His clothes seemed oppressively heavy even though he wasn't wearing a coat. He wanted to impress Sabine, show her around the city, but he felt distracted and clumsy.

She kept pace with him. They passed a smart young couple with a pram, the man fair, the woman with hair as dark as Sabine's.

"So you've decided to look after me now?"

"What would Farkas say if anything happened to you? I might get the sack."

"You could start shooting people again."

"Be careful. I might start with the person who made me lose my job."

Holland's intention was to steer Sabine towards the posher streets on the south of the Liffey. He imagined them somewhere sharing a pot of tea and eating cake, but Sabine kept veering off, taking them deeper into the dark network of back streets with their second-hand clothes' shops, tenements and barefooted children. They walked past places that could hardly be described as shops. In one, only a few heads of cabbage in the window proclaimed that anything could be bought. As they passed a butcher's, they saw a group of old women in shawls standing around a wooden barrel. Sabine stopped out of curiosity. One of the women fished out a large pink piece of flesh, with fat crumbling off the edges. She examined her catch minutely; to Sabine it looked like part of a human being, a baby's rump.

"What is *that*?" she asked Holland.

He shrugged. "Pig's cheeks. They throw them into a pot with a bit of cabbage and a few potatoes. It's very nourishing."

"People eat those things? The woman's hands are black."

"That's how the poor live here."

They wandered through the streets, their arms occasionally brushing together, unsure as to who was leading the way. And somehow, an instant at a time, Holland began to feel contentment grow inside him.

They walked down Mary's Lane past back-to-back clothes' shops; poorly dressed women toiling over heaps of used clothes.

"Why do you want to go this way?" Holland asked.

"No reason."

"We're heading to the place where I live," he added nervously, succumbing to shyness.

"I know," Sabine said.

"How do you know that?"

"We know much more about you than you think." She smiled enigmatically. "Does it make any difference to you that I am Jewish?" She gave him one of her searching looks.

"Why should it make any difference?"

"That's a very Irish answer. Answer one question with another. My parents and my brother still live in Germany. I am worried about them. I received one of my own letters back today. *Unbekannt verzogen* it said." Her voice changed pitch. "That means they departed without leaving a forwarding address. Do you understand?"

"What does it mean?"

"It means that I have lost them, until they contact me again, if they can. I had hoped they would be able to get to England."

"Could they not come to Ireland?"

"That's impossible. Your Mr de Valera has *made* it impossible."

"Is it really that bad over there? For the Jews I mean."

She seemed suddenly very grown-up to Holland.

"Perhaps some time I will tell you what it is like. You understand, I am just trying to explain my behaviour this afternoon. I saw the poster for this man who was to speak for the fascists in Spain and it made me so *wild*."

"There must be some way you can get your family out. Is Farkas helping you?"

She nodded and gave him a quick smile. "I'm hungry. Is there a good place to eat near here?"

"Depends what you want to eat."

"Anything. Eggs."

"The best aytin' house is Conroy's on Benburb Street. It'll take us a few minutes to get there."

"Let's go. As long as they don't serve pig's cheeks."

Sabine was the only female guest in the restaurant. In her fashionable clothes she couldn't have looked more out of place, but she didn't seem to notice the stares of the rest of the clientele, most of whom were cattlemen.

"Do you think I could have stirred eggs," she asked the waitress, "with toast?"

The waitress looked confused.

"Do you want scrambled eggs, Sabine?" Holland asked.

Sabine nodded.

Holland looked up at the waitress: "Scrambled eggs and toast and a cup of tea and toast for me."

When she had gone, Holland said: "Stirred eggs! Isn't that what it is in German? *Roo-eye*, or something?"

"Röhrei. You're learning the language. Why?"

"Maybe it's to spy on you."

Sabine was serious. "I wouldn't advise it. Farkas has some dangerous friends. If they knew you had information, they might come after you. For your own good, it's best to know as little as possible."

"Sabine, I'm sick of being told about all the dangers of knowing too much. To be honest, I could do with the excitement. Anyway, this is Ireland. What's there to be scared of? We don't even have real fascists any more."

When they had finished eating, Holland persuaded her to let him pay the bill. They took the tram together back to Rathmines, but Sabine insisted on making her own way home. After they had parted, Holland sat in the car, smoking, his eyes following the movement of a rainbow in the oily scum of the gutter.

8

The following Monday, Holland and Caffrey were sitting in the corner of Bewley's Café on Grafton Street. McDaid arrived and took a chair from a neighbouring table.

"Have you a proper cigarette for me, Caffrey? I've no taste for Holland's spittle."

Caffrey handed him a cigarette and winked at Holland.

They sat there smoking, McDaid lecturing as usual on some obscure aspect of Irish history.

"I have to go to the jacks," Caffrey said.

As soon as he had gone, McDaid moved closer to Holland. "That boyo; it's a wonder he's in the Movement at all. He has about as much political belief as a dose of ringworm."

"On the other hand, as you've said yourself, if you're in a tight spot, there's no better man to be with."

"You're right. I suppose he's the most reliable volunteer I've got. But you have to wonder about his motivation. What the hell made him join? Do *you* know? Is it just for kicks?"

Holland did not respond, regarding McDaid's question as rhetorical.

McDaid continued: "Well, as you say, he's a good soldier. He always does what he's told, even if he makes smart-alecky remarks all the time."

"A couple of hundred like him and we'd have the British on the run."

McDaid produced a wintry smile. He lowered his voice. "Will I tell you who our worst enemy is? It's not the Free Staters or the British Empire. They can be beaten. And it's not the informers; we can handle them if we're careful and carry out the proper procedures." He leant back in his chair and stared at Holland for added effect. "The real enemy is the collection of incompetent arse-holes who make up about fifty or sixty per cent of any organisation like ours. They're blocks of granite around our necks. They mean well—that's the worst of it—but when all's said and done, they do far more harm than the Black and Tans ever did. And you know what?" His mouth moved towards Holland's ear and his voice dropped to a whisper. "You're never allowed to shoot the fuckers, no matter how many cock-ups they're respon-sible for."

McDaid gave Holland a cool look.

"You're the dark horse, aren't you?"

The colour drained from Holland's face. "What do you mean, Boss?"

"I've heard about you and the *bean an tí*. You put on this chaste act with the women and all the time… you know what I'm talking about. It's a dangerous game, Holland. There's some who think it deserves the severest punishment. Personally—"

"I don't know what you heard, but it's not true."

McDaid's eyes turned icy. Without as much as changing his position, his body suddenly threatened Holland. "Don't make me into a fool, Holland. If I have to defend you and it turns out you lied to me…." He clicked his fingers. "You're this far away from a court martial."

Holland lowered his head; he could feel red-hot blood coursing into his face.

"Oh yes, I know more about you than you think. But I'm looking out for you."

"What do you want me to do? Move?"

McDaid smiled, in command again. "Bad idea. Suspicious. Stay where you are for the time being. There's only one witness and he's mine."

Caffrey returned from the toilet.

"Holly, you look as if someone's been walking over your grave."

McDaid grinned: "We've been chatting about the facts of life."

"You mean, get your shot in before the other guy."

"Something like that," McDaid said, casting his eyes toward Holland.

Holland ignored him and glanced over at the entrance. A young woman had just walked in and before he had time to direct his gaze at anything else, Holland realised that he was looking straight at Sabine. She had changed clothes and was now wearing a navy-blue tailored suit. Her hair was severely pinned back on her head. From a distance it looked as if she had a black helmet on her head. He wondered if she had a date but, instead of looking around, she walked directly over to their table. Holland was taken aback.

McDaid stood up as she approached.

"Excuse me, are you Mr McGuire?" she asked. McDaid nodded and Sabine continued: "I have something for you."

She handed McDaid an envelope and he asked her to sit down with them. Holland fetched an extra chair.

"Could I tempt you with a cup of something?"

Sabine asked for a coffee and McDaid raised an arm lazily in the air to attract a waitress.

"Thanks again for saving me the other day," Sabine said to Holland.

Holland's face reddened and McDaid squinted at him. "I didn't know our friend here was a hero. Aren't you going to present the young lady to us?"

"Sabine, you know Mr McGuire, and this is a friend of mine, Mick Byrne," he said.

"Are you brothers?"

McDaid laughed.

"We're all brothers, you might say."

Holland realised that he had used one of Caffrey's old cover names out of habit.

"You can call them blood brothers," McDaid interjected. "You know of course that Byrne is a very common name in these parts. Like Smith in England."

"How do you all know each other?"

"You could say we all know each other through the same club," said McDaid. "Only we have branched out a bit on our own—in the same business of course."

"What sort of club is it?"

Holland felt queasy. McDaid was enjoying himself too much. Being a foreigner, Sabine was of no importance to him.

McDaid narrowed his eyes and pouted. "We're members of the same plant lovers' society. We want to reintroduce the native wild plants and eradicate the varieties introduced by the British. It's a lifelong occupation. There's no let up. I suppose you could call us ... enthusiasts."

Sabine was puzzled. "What if the new varieties are more useful? You can't just get rid of everything because it is new."

"In my experience, none of the new varieties are of any use whatsoever. They have no right to be here. Although I'm not saying that all the old varieties are equally good. Some of them might have to go too. It's a root and branch process; it's not easy work but someone has to do it."

He smiled benignly at Sabine. Holland could sense her mind sorting through different options to reach a conclusion.

"I know what you are," she declared suddenly. She moved her head backwards as if to view all three of them together as one unit. "You're the nationalists… Republicans. And you" —she looked at McDaid— "you're their leader. Is that not true?"

McDaid laughed so much, he started to cough. "Is it true? Isn't it just? Keep it quiet, girl, or they'll be carting us away in chains."

A waitress arrived with their coffee. Caffrey and Holland lit their cigarettes and Caffrey began to talk about football to change the subject. But Sabine was unwilling to let go.

"I do not understand why there is any conflict here. You have everything: your own government, democracy, and your own army. You can do what you want in this country."

Holland thought that McDaid might lose his temper, but he was in one of his avuncular moods—and Sabine was an outsider. His mouth tightened and his eyes creased shut as though he were deep in thought.

"It's just an illusion," he said. "This is really a puppet state belonging to Britain. When London pulls the strings, the people here start jigging about."

"What about de Valera? He is a Republican. How can you say he is just doing what the British want?"

"Like so many others, he's a turncoat."

"A turncoat?"

"A traitor," Holland explained.

McDaid was growing tired of arguing about the present and retreated to the safety of the past—the deep well of injustice that provided the nationalist with all the rationalisation he needed. He begged another cigarette from Caffrey and turned his head away from them to light it.

"Traitors," he said, drawing the smoke into his mouth, "is what Irish history is all about. We've always had them. Owen Roe O'Neill—you've probably never heard of him. He was the greatest leader we Irish ever had. He commanded armies on the Continent: he beat every English army that came near him, matter a damn how poorly trained his troops were. He could have stopped Cromwell in his tracks and saved Gaelic Ireland. But what happened to him? Just before Cromwell landed with his troops, an informer—a filthy traitor—paid by the English, put poison in his wine. In my own county too."

"Was he a friend of this man Patrick Pearse?" Sabine asked innocently.

"He might as well have been, girl," McDaid replied wearily. "He might as well have been."

Holland said: "This didn't happen in 1916, Sabine, it happened nearly three hundred years ago."

"That was the informer who brought old Ireland down," McDaid continued, "Now if we could only build a time machine like that fellow Wells dreamt up, we could send someone back to put a bullet through that traitor's head."

"And if you did, perhaps none of us would ever have existed," Sabine said brightly.

"Ah, but it would be worth it, wouldn't it? We would have to make the end justify the means, wouldn't we?"

Sabine finished her coffee and stood up to leave.

"Thank you for speaking to me. I have to get back to Mr Farkas."

Holland was surprised. "You work this late?"

"Sometimes." Sabine straightened her clothes. "It was nice to meet you."

McDaid watched her through hooded eyes as she left.

"Smart as a whip, that one. I wouldn't say she's scared of a thing. You know, I'd be wary of what I say to her, Holland. She could put the wind up a busload of bishops."

"According to Mincey, we should be putting all the bishops up against a wall," Caffrey said.

"Mightn't do them any harm," McDaid replied. "Poor old Mincey. Did he see any action in Spain?"

"I heard he shot half-a-dozen priests and a bishop, and raped a convent full of nuns."

"The priests and the bishop I might take, but raping the nuns? Poor old Mincey's more likely to get raped himself."

Caffrey began to talk about some of the other volunteers Mincey had fought with in Spain but McDaid was only half listening. He opened the letter Sabine had given him and started to read. When he had finished, he put it carefully into the inside pocket of his jacket and slapped both hands on the table.

"Tomorrow evening we're going for a little trip into the mountains. Holland, you have permission to take Farkas' car from the lockout. Pick it up at seven and collect myself and Caffrey. We'll wait for you across from *An Phoblacht* on St Andrew Street. I'll give you directions from there. Oh yes, bring along short arms."

Caffrey was annoyed. "I'm supposed to be giving weapons' training tomorrow evening."

"This is more important. You'll just have to cancel it. I need you with me tomorrow. Anyway, lads, I have to be going." He pulled on his coat, a large heavy garment of Galway frieze, and placed a couple of shillings on the table. "Remember, seven o'clock sharp and no word of it to anybody."

9

The following evening was foul. Rain fell in thick grey sheets. Holland cursed his lack of a hat as he walked, half-blinded by the downpour. He picked up the car and drove the short distance to St Andrew Street. Caffrey and McDaid were sheltering together as best they could in the entrance of a shop. Caffrey was holding an umbrella and McDaid had a briefcase partially obscured by his coat. They shook themselves vigorously like dogs before getting into the back of the car.

Holland said: "I'll need to get some petrol if we're going far."

"Fair enough," said McDaid. "We're all right for time."

Holland took a left turn on Dame Street. Buses loomed up above them like ships sailing through the rain.

"It's a nice machine this," McDaid said. "A fella could get used to this kind of luxury."

Holland headed west up the Lucan Road where he knew there was an Esso station that stayed open late. A small thin man wearing spectacles ran out from the shelter and began to fill the tank without having to be asked. Holland was by now a regular customer. When he'd finished, Holland wound down the window and handed him the money. The man had no coat on and his clothes were drenched. There was so much rain running down the lenses of his glasses, it looked as if his eyes were under water. Holland took pity on him and slipped him an extra threepenny bit.

"You're a soft-hearted eejit," said McDaid from the back. "He's probably a Fine Gael Blueshirt on his day off."

"Where are we going, Boss?" Holland asked.

"Head for Blessington. I'll tell you where to go from there."

Even with the wipers working full blast, Holland had difficulty finding the right road. Caffrey lit a couple of cigarettes and placed one in Holland's mouth. The inside of the car became warm and humid and Holland had to keep wiping the windscreen with a cloth to stop it from fogging up.

They turned south-east at Blessington and began to drive into the Wicklow uplands. Mountains rose harsh and black on either side. Holland concentrated on the thin triangles of yellow light cutting open the darkness in front of the car. After twenty-five minutes he noticed some kind of illumination ahead, feebly wavering above them in the gloomy skies.

"This is the place," McDaid announced. "There's a pub on the left. You can pull in there."

They drove through a village consisting of a single street with a couple of shops and a tiny church at one end. There was a pub, barely distinguishable from the other buildings, with a high-gabled slate roof. The rain had eased but Holland felt the chill of the mountain air as soon as he stepped out of the car.

"Doesn't look as if they've arrived yet," McDaid said. "We'll go inside and get something to warm our innards."

Half-a-dozen men were arranged in various poses around the counter of the pub. There were condiments and tins on the shelves closest to the door. McDaid, who appeared to know the publican, a low stocky man, exchanged a few words with him and ordered hot whiskies. They sat around a table. No one paid any attention to them, which in such a small place seemed peculiar to Holland.

"Who are we waiting for?" Holland asked finally.

"Questions, questions." McDaid shook his head. "I'm telling you this for your own good—it's best not to know."

Their drinks arrived. McDaid's eyes ranged over the silent men at the bar. His fingers drummed a nervous beat on the table. They heard some honky-tonk music from a room behind the counter.

"Tin Pan Alley," spluttered McDaid. "That kind of music shouldn't be allowed on the wireless."

Caffrey laughed: "With all due respect, jazz is the best music if you want to get off with someone. How the hell do you get a woman in the humour if you play *The Goose is in the Praties*, or start prancing around with your hands glued to your sides?"

"Jazz is just nigger music. There shouldn't be any place for it in a country like Ireland," McDaid said primly.

The barman made a sign to McDaid.

"They're here. Holland, you stay outside and keep an eye on the road. If it gets too cold, you can sit in the car. Caffrey, you come with me."

Holland watched the two men follow the barman behind the bar and through a narrow doorway. He finished his drink and walked outside. The rain had stopped, but the wind had a sharp edge to it. He walked to the crest of the hill that marked the middle of the village. The road was swallowed up by the night at either end.

From where he was standing, he could clearly see the only other car on the street, parked in the shadow of a house about fifty yards from the pub. It was quite new and gleamed brassily even in the slender light emanating from the few houses on the street. He guessed that it belonged to whomever McDaid was talking to. While he was standing there, he heard footsteps approaching from behind. Before turning around, he slipped his right hand into his pocket and gathered his house keys into the ball of his fist. It was the only weapon available; he had left the Parabellum in the car. A tall, heavily built man was walking towards him.

When he was a few yards away, the man smiled broadly and lifted up his arms as if to slow down his approach and indicate his good intentions.

"So, you are a tourist here too," he said in strongly accented English.

"I'm just minding my business." It struck Holland that this was not exactly the place or the time of year one would expect to meet a foreign tourist.

The man laughed. His hair was cropped so short that Holland thought he was bald until a beam of stray light picked out the stubble on his head.

"Whatever you say. It is a cold night, no? May I offer a cigarette?"

Holland loosened his grip on the keys and took his hand out of his pocket to accept one. The stranger lit his cigarette and they tactfully observed each other under the sharp explosion of red and white light from the man's lighter.

The foreigner coughed. "This lighter, you know, it's made from a used magazine. From the Great War." He handed it to Holland so that he could examine it. "I use it to impress women. They like toys like that."

"Where are you from?"

"Ah, you don't know?" The man suddenly looked perturbed. Holland took pity on him.

65

"It's all right. I'm with our friends inside the pub. I'm not the police."

The man took an extra hard drag on his cigarette. "I begin to worry who you are. Hey, it's not wise we stand here in the middle of the road. We can go over to the car."

They strolled over to the shadows. "My name's Rodolf. I'm from the Netherlands. You know I like it in this country. The weather is wet and cold, but you have plenty of space. Not like at home. Here, you can build where you want but have not the technique. We Dutch have the technique—factories all over—but no room to build."

Holland remembered the reports he had read in the newspapers at Mundial Financing. Rodolf's speech sounded like Tarzan's version of the Nazi argument.

"It's too cold to be out the whole time. We can divide the work. I can spend half-an-hour on watch, then you spend half-an-hour. Yes?"

And that is how they split their time. Holland curled up in the back of the Wolseley until Rodolf knocked on the window. Between shifts they chatted. After about two hours, McDaid and Caffrey emerged from the pub and waved to Holland, who happened to be standing in the street. Holland knocked on the door of the Dutchman's car and walked over to the Wolseley. Both McDaid and Caffrey looked exhausted.

"Tough customers to deal with," McDaid said. They climbed gratefully into the car. Caffrey sighed and flopped into the corner of the backseat. "Home, James!" he said. Holland started the engine, made a tight turn, and drove them back towards the welcoming lights of Dublin.

10

One evening, about a week after the Wicklow trip, Farkas rang Holland at his digs and asked him to come to the office.

Holland crossed the Liffey and walked the rest of the way to the office faster than he was used to. He was surprised to run into his employer on the stairs, but Farkas was clearly relieved to see him.

"I have no time to explain. I need you to come with me to London," he said. "I have an extra toothbrush, shaving gear."

"How long are we going to be there?" Holland was desperately trying to remember if he had made any arrangements for the following days.

"Just a day or two. You can send a note to your landlady. We'll be catching the mail boat."

They walked to the lock-up. Farkas placed a leather suitcase in the boot and Holland carefully steered the car out of the city centre, avoiding the jolting tram tracks as best he could. They drove past St Stephen's Green. Holland found Farkas' eyes in the mirror.

"Would it be possible to drop off a note in Rathmines? I was supposed to go there this evening."

Farkas checked his watch and nodded.

"Make it quick."

Holland pulled up in front of a Republican safe house on York Street, quickly scribbled a note and left it with the owner. The note was addressed to McDaid: Holland informed him that he was leaving the country but would be back in a few days. Twenty minutes later they pulled up beside the ferry building in Dun Laoghaire. Farkas bought their tickets and they boarded the ship ahead of most of the other passengers.

"Have you sailed first-class before?" Farkas asked as they climbed the gangway.

"I've never sailed any class before: I've never been outside the country."

Farkas was amused. "Then I feel obliged to make this trip pleasant for you. The surface of the sea is as calm as a lake. That will help."

Holland looked dubiously at the grey waves dashing against the pier.

Farkas led the way to the first-class saloon and ordered brandies from a white-coated steward. They found seats and talked about the political situation on the Continent. Thanks to the newspapers in the office, Holland was reasonably well informed. He even felt bold enough to make a few general comments.

Farkas seemed to be impressed by his opinions, as if observing Holland fully for the first time.

"Now I would imagine you are not a man who gives any support to the fascists. Am I correct?"

Holland nodded.

"Well, I am of the same mind of course. But I have to work with the authorities in Germany, to some extent at least, to carry out some of my business transactions."

"And what sort of transactions might they be?"

Farkas' voice became instantly conspiratorial. "There are a great number of wealthy people in Germany, you understand: people who are unwished for, people who are desperately trying to escape. And it is getting more and more difficult to obtain visas for them. It is permitted for the children to emigrate, but then they have no money to support them in the new country. And they try to get their parents out too. My role is to facilitate the movement of papers of value, securities, promissory notes, obligations and so on. These assets are liquefied and can provide an income either here or in America— for the children who escape, at least."

"And then you take your cut?"

"Of course; we must cover our expenses. But there is an element of risk on our side. By going to England, for instance, I am taking a small, additional risk and I need to know that you are behind me. If you feel that this exceeds your… remit; that is perfectly in order. I can only insist that you accompany me as far as London."

Farkas gave Holland a naked look, before puffing nervously on his cigarette.

It became clear to Holland that Farkas was afraid. He had to know to what extent he could rely on his chauffeur. Holland suddenly understood the necessity of the Parabellum, the unusually generous perks, the unnecessarily high wages. It had all been leading up to this: would you risk your life to protect mine? Would you kill to save my life?

Holland looked into the warm tan centre of the brandy, the little waves that reflected the large slowly swelling tons of water upon which the ship rode.

"If what you say is true, I will protect you," Holland said. "If not, I won't feel obliged to do anything."

Farkas smiled wearily but seemed satisfied. "You are very honourable," he said quietly. "I respect that. I am also a man of honour, although many choose not to believe this. Honour is personal too. It involves discovering what it is exactly people are committed to, and what they are prepared to do about it. Everyone has his own individual pattern. For instance, I could have offered you extra money, but I knew that would have been a mistake." As if struck by a sudden feeling of self-consciousness, having said too much, Farkas sprang to his feet. Ash from his cigarette sprayed over Holland's suit. "I am forgetting my manners! Allow me to order us another drink before we have something to eat."

They spent the next few hours eating, drinking and chatting. All the time Holland's mind kept returning to thoughts of London. He still imagined it as it was featured in the propaganda tracts of the Movement: he had heard it described as a giant spider, grown fat on the blood of its minions, suspended within the vast web-like network of the British Empire. It was difficult for him to imagine it as a real place, with streets of brick houses, pubs and landmarks, and ordinary people thronging its pavements.

The boat was full of emigrants, although Holland was aware of them only as a distant throng. The majority were young people from the countryside, fresh-faced and ignorant of the world, cardboard suitcases containing the pathetic reminders of their past. There was no foothold for any of them in this farcical Free State, thought Holland. In a few months they would have English clothes and be labouring on English roads or working in English factories.

By the time Holland and Farkas had finished their lunch, and retired to the first-class lounge, the Welsh coast had begun to appear as a grey smudge on the horizon. They entered Holyhead harbour. There was no sense of occasion or drama as the engine slowed to half-speed and then stopped, and the ferry drifted sideways in against the quayside. One had the sense that this was normality, that

this grey town was the rim of the everyday world, and
Ireland a country of the mind, a mirage on the opposite
side of the sea.

As the passengers started to disembark, Holland
could feel his body tense. It suddenly occurred to him
that Farkas might have been rash enough to stash a handgun in his suitcase. If the customs officers found it, they
would also be able to discover his true identity and that
would probably mean a long prison term.

But if Farkas had any thoughts of the risk involved,
he showed no sign of it. He marched through customs,
his head held high, lightly badgering his chauffeur about
the importance of keeping up with him and minding
his luggage. Holland noticed a medium-sized man in
a dark coat standing behind the customs officers. His
eyes passed over all the passengers with studied indiffer-
ence, although it was clear he was alert to every detail,
every nuance. It was not an altogether unfriendly gaze.
It seemed to Holland almost as if he were looking for a
relative or close friend and that he might emerge from
the shadows and throw his arms about any man or
woman who fitted the description. His eyes flitted lazily
over Holland's face and, disappointed, continued sadly
over the faces of the people behind. The other officers looked him up and down but since it was obvious
that he was with Farkas, and that Farkas was a gentle-
man, they let him pass unhindered. They walked past
the immigrants, men in cheap suits and women wearing print dresses and hand-knitted cardigans. Socks and
shirts spilled out of cardboard suitcases as the customs
men delved through them, their disgust almost tangible.
Within a matter of seconds Farkas and he were through
and out on the other side. For the first time, Holland
was standing on the island of Britain. The air smelled

the same, the temperature was the same, the people looked much the same.

"Come on, please. The train won't wait for us," Farkas urged.

Within half-an-hour they were comfortably installed in their first-class carriage, inspecting the Welsh country-side as it rolled past.

"Here I am back in this boring, intolerable place. All the English can think of is money and status. They have no interest in developments on the Continent. I have a feeling they'll be in for a big surprise if they are not care-ful."

In Holland's eyes Britain looked wealthy, populous and incredibly well organised. In Ireland, shabbiness and decay seemed everywhere to be the dominant impression. But here, every public building, each street and railway station seemed to have achieved a toylike aura of orderli-ness and cleanliness. The people he could see, far off, or collected in the stations they passed through, appeared to be inhabited by a sense of purpose, content with their lot. The feeling of inner chaos and public unruliness that affected even the least politically motivated citizens in Ireland did not seem to exist. The countryside was tidy here, copses and fields regularly spaced as though planned that way by a higher authority.

They arrived at Euston Station early the following morning. During the night Farkas had awoken in a panic and grabbed Holland's arm as he lay in his bunk.

"You will not abandon me? No matter what. You will not abandon me? Say you won't!"

Holland stared into eyes that were wild with fright. He shook himself awake, wondering if someone had burst into their compartment.

"Easy now. There's no danger."

Farkas fell back as if the air had been knocked out of him.

"A dream, a nightmare. Just a dream," he said and returned to his bunk.

Neither of them could sleep. They smoked cigarettes and began to talk. Holland asked Farkas if he'd been in the Great War.

"I was on the Eastern Front."

"What was it like?"

"Not possible to describe. In the West you had armies that at least had the same sort of physical…" Farkas struggled with his words, "techniques, equipment. In the east, half the Russians had no rifles, no weapons of any kind, not even boots on their feet. You can't imagine what it was like… we were shooting directly into great herds of running men."

"What was the idea of sending men in without guns?"

"There were so many casualties. They took guns from their own dead. You did them a favour by shooting them. You supplied their comrades with arms."

Farkas went silent. Holland imagined him remembering the carnage and decided to keep him talking.

"But how could it have done any good attacking like that?"

"Usually it didn't, but sometimes they made it through the machine-gun fire, the barbed wire, the bombardments—you know many of them were barefoot, you can imagine, eh?—but if once they made it through and breached a trench in force, our men had no chance. The Russians tore them apart with their bare hands. You must understand: instead of having proper equipment, artillery, machine guns, the Russians had the bodies of their men. You could say a thousand men was the equivalent of so many tons of barbed wire or a couple of machine guns.

If you killed a thousand men, they were simply replaced, just as you would replace an artillery piece."

Farkas finished his cigarette and got out of his bunk to stub it out in the ashtray by the window. He pulled back the tiny curtains and looked out; the lights of distant factories shone blue-white through the black countryside like columns of burning ice.

"One wonders what purpose that war served. Do you know Luger's eldest son died in one of those attacks? A fine officer. Our own artillery killed him. A mistake."

"Is that where you got the scar? In the war?"

Farkas laughed. "No, it was from *die Mensur*, a kind of duelling club at university. A ridiculous affectation." He climbed back into his bunk. "Thank you for bearing with me. You have been a great help."

Holland extinguished his cigarette and, as the train raced through the middle of England, they both managed to find comfort in sleep.

London was huge and bustling. When they arrived, its streets were crowded with serious-minded people on their way to work. Holland examined the faces of the English with interest. They walked faster and more purposefully, and they were better and more fashionably dressed. However hard he tried, he could not see them as enemies of Ireland; in fact, he began to suspect that Dublin was nothing but a distant suburb pulsing with the same energy that came from this great beating heart.

Farkas was back to his old self. Now it was Holland who felt vulnerable and uncertain. They took a taxi to Mundial's London offices, situated in a backstreet in Soho. Another secretary—unlike Sabine, she was fair-haired—took Farkas aside as soon as they arrived. There was an important message. Farkas went into a room and made two phone calls. He returned paler and more agitated.

"We need to hire a motor car." He looked at the secretary. "Please arrange it. Immediately!"

The secretary practically hopped out of her seat.

"Where are we going?" Holland asked.

Farkas looked startled, as though surprised that Holland was still with him. "We have a meeting... in the countryside."

They took a taxi to a garage near Clapham Common to pick up the car. It was a brand new Morris 8, reliable but not in the least flashy. Holland speculated that Farkas wanted something as anonymous as possible. With a road map on his lap, he directed Holland towards the Great West Road and away from London. The traffic was dense and the street signs difficult to interpret. Holland drove nervously. The pedestrian crossings and traffic lights were quite new to him: the first time he approached the Belisha beacons, he had to ask Farkas what they were. But if Farkas noticed his anxiety, he didn't say anything.

The city streets gradually disappeared, but instead of fields and countryside, they found themselves surrounded by a continuous line of new factories on either side of the road. Holland had never seen anything like them before. Constructed of glass and chromium plate, they seemed to hang in the air like the painted palaces from a pantomime.

The sheer volume of traffic also impressed Holland: within an hour he saw more cars than he would have seen in a month in Dublin. The drivers were aggressive. Many of them drove at speed and overtook other cars whenever they felt like it. When Holland deftly pulled in sharply to allow one of these oncoming cars to pass, Farkas looked at him approvingly and commented: "What I like about you, Byrne, is your calmness and foresight. It gives me strength. It steadies my hand."

"Have you never thought of learning to drive yourself?"

"I can drive perfectly well. I enjoyed driving before the war. Since that time I have never cared for it. My mind is not concentrated. I would be a hazard."

"You've seen some things," Holland stated matter-of-factly.

Farkas livened up. His brown eyes danced. "Do you know, I sometimes have the strange idea that I was actually one of the dead and that this world is my reward. Queer eh? All the men I saw die; they, in reality, are the ones who survived. Perhaps there are two universes, and everyone gets a chance to become old."

"A bit hard to prove."

After driving for about an hour, they stopped at a roadhouse near Camberley for something to eat. Despite the modest car, the manager came out in person and attended to them as if they were noblemen passing through on some great quest. His obsequiousness irritated Holland, but Farkas was amused. When their host had gone to fetch their food, he said conspiratorially: "Ah, the English. The right air and the right appearance and they will lick your boots. Members of the lower middle classes, such as this creature here, are the worst. 'Conscious of the marks of his servitude' as one of your English poets has said."

"I'm not English."

"Of course not, but can you deny that your language is English?" said Farkas, his left eyebrow raised.

Holland felt the *fáinne* on his lapel and said nothing.

When they had finished their meal—an uninteresting concoction of stew and mashed potatoes—paid the bill and returned to the car, Farkas asked Holland to open the glove compartment. Holland found the tips of his fingers caressing the cold surface of a Parabellum pistol.

"Before you ask; no, I didn't smuggle your gun into England. This is one I have kept hidden in my London office. I put it there when you were buying cigarettes."

"I should take a look at it. They're delicate instruments. If they haven't been cleaned properly, they tend to jam."

"I doubt we'll need it. It's just good to know it's there, as security."

Farkas still wouldn't tell Holland exactly where they were going or who they were to meet.

"The less you know, the better it is for your health," he said, and Holland—who was used to hearing the same platitudes from McDaid—did not push the matter.

About ten minutes outside Camberley, Farkas directed him down a number of minor roads. After half-an-hour of negotiating these and passing through villages with names ending in 'holt' and 'heath', Farkas asked him to drive down a narrow lane ending in a field. Holland noticed that at some point his employer had exchanged the road atlas for a small-scale ordinance survey map.

"This is the spot. We are a little early. Our friends shall not be here for another hour."

"Where will they park their car? If they park behind us, they'll block our way out of here."

"Ever the soldier, Mr Byrne. I'll meet them in that large flat field over there, out in the open. There's another lane on the other side; you can see the gate. No one's escape route will be blocked."

The hour passed with inexorable slowness. Holland scouted around the woods on each side of the field while Farkas looked through his papers. The place had been well chosen. There was little sign of any agricultural activity. According to Farkas, the farm was up for sale, like so many others in the vicinity. If Holland met anyone, he was to tell them that they were looking the place over.

Under the protective branches of a small stand of beech trees, Holland checked and tested the pistol as well as he could without firing. There was only one magazine and it seemed a little loose, as if it had received a blow at some point. The eight bullets were all there: he weighed each one in his hand and hoped that they hadn't been sitting in a drawer in Farkas' office for too long. Without the right tools, it was impossible to do any more. He stuck the gun into his belt and prayed to God that he would not have to use it.

On his way back to the car, Holland noticed a metallic flash from the far side of the field. He wondered whether the people they were to meet were scouting around too before showing themselves.

At three o'clock exactly, two men walked into the middle of the field from the other side. They were of medium height and wore long grey coats. One was bareheaded—his fair hair caught the light—while the other, who appeared to be in charge, wore a trilby. Farkas collected his papers and told Holland to keep as much out of sight as possible. Then he went out into the field to meet them. There was no hint of the terror which had stalked him the previous night.

Fifteen minutes went by while they talked. Holland sat in the car smoking cigarettes and watching them. Then he returned to the beech trees that flanked the left side of the field. The ground was so uneven that he could easily approach without being seen. He was now about a hundred yards from where they were standing but, besides a wave of fragmented sound, he could hear nothing of their conversation.

As he watched, the man with the trilby suddenly became very agitated, as though Farkas had said something rash. There was a scuffle. The blond man grabbed the papers Farkas was holding and handed them to his accomplice. Farkas stepped backwards and looked as if he was considering making a run for it, but something kept him from moving. Holland saw what it was: the blond man had pulled a carbine from under his coat. He jammed the gun into Farkas' neck and forced him to his knees. The man with the trilby began to study the papers he had been handed as if Farkas' predicament was now of no importance to him.

Holland took out the Parabellum and released the safety catch. Unable to decide what to do, he waited, his right arm trembling violently.

Having finished reading whatever was in Farkas' papers, the trilby man threw them to the ground. His fist struck the side of Farkas' face. He then looked at the blond thug and nodded abruptly. The henchman pointed his gun directly at Farkas' head, and Holland—instinctively—fired a shot in the air, left the cover of the trees and stepped into the field. As his feet touched the spongy grass, Holland wondered if this would be the place where he would die.

The trilby man shouted an order, took out his own gun and trained it on Farkas. The blond man began to move towards Holland. He walked slowly as if intent on not scaring away his target. At first he didn't even bother to raise his gun. About seventy yards separated them, not a good distance for an accurate shot with a Parabellum. Holland lifted the pistol with both hands and pulled the trigger but there was no reaction. The blond man smiled and raised his own gun as he closed in. A bullet shot past Holland's right ear and he dropped to his knees and desperately pulled on the magazine latch. Another shot struck the ground on his right. The blond man began to move quickly now, his carbine raised ready for the kill. After a final tug, the magazine dropped into Holland's hand. He shook it and shoved it back into the butt. The blond man raised his gun to fire again and this time Holland decided to let him have the full complement. He squeezed the trigger. The Parabellum came to life and he fired five rounds in quick succession. The gun bucked in his hands, but he managed to get a good bead on his opponent for the last two rounds. The man dropped to the ground. There was shouting from where Farkas was standing. The man with the trilby was running back across the field, presumably to the place where his car was parked. Holland ran forward, passing the blond man, who lay there semi-conscious, his limbs in spasm.

Farkas was sitting in the grass clutching his papers when Holland reached him. He looked towards the far side of the field. "Damn! This is a mess. We need to stop him getting away."

"Why?"

"Don't argue. Capture him or shoot him. I'll explain later."

Holland began to lope towards the gate, but the man in the trilby had already disappeared behind the hedgerow. With only two rounds left; and no extra ammunition, he wasn't sure he could stop him anyway. At the gate, he heard the violent protests of a car engine and a roar as the wheels bit the loose gravel of the laneway. He continued to run, skirting the side of the lane, but all that was left of the car was a plume of blue smoke.

Farkas, out of breath, caught up with him a few minutes later.

"We must get away from this place."

"What about the man I hit?"

"He's not going anywhere."

Holland felt a heaviness in his stomach.

Farkas waved a pistol in front of his face. "I found this Walther in his pocket and used it for the coup de grâce. He fancied his chances as a marksman. Probably thought you were just a simple chauffeur whom he could gun down at his leisure."

"He nearly did."

They walked in silence across the great expanse of the field, aware of the corpse on the far side. Farkas had shot him in the forehead and his head rested on a morbid crown of blood and brain matter. There was blood on the leg above the right knee and a large open wound under his ribcage. He might have survived both these injuries if he had been taken to a competent doctor.

Holland knelt over the body and examined the man's pockets.

"What are you doing?" Farkas asked sharply.

"I want to see who he was."

"No need. He's a German spy: they usually don't carry identity papers."

Holland went through his pockets all the same but found nothing besides two ten shilling notes and a small number of coins. The only personal item was a small gold necklace under the man's shirt. Holland pulled on it and a small medallion popped out. The design struck Holland as familiar but he couldn't remember where he had seen it before.

Farkas said: "Take his money; it's of no use to him now. How strange the way his eyes follow you? I haven't seen a dead man this close since the war."

"Should we get rid of the body?"

"There's nothing to connect us to it. No one saw us arrive. I suggest we get away from here as quickly as possible and back to Ireland."

Before he left, Farkas picked up the carbine and placed the Walther in the man's right hand.

"They'll hardly think it was suicide," said Holland.

Farkas took a last look at the corpse. "Never underestimate the laziness of the police."

On the way back to London, they drove past a stretch of canal. Farkas asked Holland to stop the car. He picked up the carbine, went down to the edge and tossed it into the water. "Like Excalibur," he said when he got back.

In London they made a brief second visit to the Mundial office, and Farkas spoke on the phone for an hour.

They found a hotel for the night and returned to Dublin by the early mail boat the following morning. In the meantime they spoke about what had happened, although Farkas was reluctant to tell Holland more than he had to. The two men who had threatened to shoot Farkas were from the Abwehr, the German counter-intelligence service. They wanted him to work for them, but he had refused. He didn't think they would really have shot him: it wouldn't have made much sense since he was of no use to them dead. In other words, Holland's feat of bravado had been unnecessary.

"We should have finished off the second one. He'll report what happened."

"Will they come after you again?"

"I feel much safer in Ireland, thanks to you and your friends."

Holland wasn't so sure he was right.

After disembarking in Dun Laoghaire, they picked up the Wolseley and drove into the city. Despite the lateness of the hour, Farkas insisted on paying a visit to his office. He extracted a bundle of papers from a filing cabinet, put them into a satchel and asked Holland to take them back to his digs for safe keeping.

"If those papers get into the wrong hands, a lot of people will die," he said.

"What you're saying is that they'll come after me if you get plugged."

Farkas' lips drew back to form a morbid smile. "Not exactly. But if anything happens to me, just destroy them—every trace. They're not interested in you. Unfortunately, these papers also represent my livelihood, so I cannot destroy them immediately. Sabine's family is named there. I know you are interested in her welfare." He slipped the last sentence in as though it were an afterthought. He had said it, but he might just as well have chosen not to say it. The words struck Holland like a smack in the face.

"Why should I be interested in your secretary's family?" His voice was brittle.

Farkas looked cannily at him. "Don't be so surprised. I know a lot more about you than you think. You cannot say that you have been terribly discreet."

Holland's mind raced back. Could he have been followed on the day he extricated Sabine from the angry mob in Rathmines?

"You were hand-picked, Holland. Do you think I would have chosen just anybody to be my chauffeur? Your name suits you. No heights or depths. You think logically in straight lines. And, most importantly, you are an honourable man. I like that. You will look after Sabine if anything happens to me?"

Holland nodded, barely aware that Farkas had used his real name for the first time.

"Good. Now we must get moving. Take these papers and hide them somewhere safe. I have other business to attend to, and it is best done alone."

11

The following morning, a note arrived for Holland. Mrs Mullen handed it to him at the foot of the stairs on the way to breakfast. At first, he thought that it might have been a personal message from Mrs Mullen, but the writing was too masculine. There was no sender's name or address. It stated that he should not go to work today, since Farkas was no longer 'available'. Instead of going to the office, he was to be at O'Hanlon's Corner at ten o'clock, where he would receive further notification. 'Notification' was McDaid's favourite euphemism for orders. He folded the note and carefully put it into the inside pocket of his jacket.

At the breakfast table, the other lodgers talked about the weather and a Gaelic football match that had been played on the previous Sunday, but Holland could not concentrate on anything they said. The word 'available' nagged at him. Had the Germans caught up with Farkas or had he gone to McDaid for protection? He thought either possibility unlikely: it sounded more as if Farkas had decided to fly the coop. He pictured Sabine arriving punctually at nine o'clock, unsuspecting. They might be waiting for her at the entrance of the building or more likely somewhere on the stairs. She would be pushed into the back of a car, a revolver or a knife discreetly pointed at her ribs. If Farkas had disappeared, as he guessed, they would probably take her to a remote place and attempt

to extract information from her. Her stubbornness—
he could easily imagine her defiant looks as they grilled
her—would only make matters worse.

He found his coat and left. In less than a minute, he
knew he was being followed. There was at least one man
behind him and another farther up the street. He was
careful not to give any indication that he was on to them,
pretending instead to be going to work as usual.

He stopped in front of a shop window and examined
the street behind him. A young man in a trench coat stood
about twenty yards to his right, his image oddly flattened
by the glass. He was staring directly at Holland's back, not
making the least effort to conceal himself. Holland rolled
up the note from McDaid and jettisoned it as he pushed
his way through a group of women carrying washing.
When the women began to cross the street, he darted
into a lane and began to run. It would have been a good
plan if the Special Branch detectives had been less interested in him. Holland didn't know that in addition to the
man in the trench coat, who was meant to flush him out,
there were at least four other detectives tailing him.

The chase lasted less than a minute. They cornered
him before he could reach a crowded shopping street or
make a last desperate dash for the Liffey. They were all
armed. He raised his hands and gave up without a struggle. One of the men searched his pockets and extracted
his wallet: there was nothing inside to identify him. A car
pulled up directly in front of them, almost riding over
the feet of the detectives closest to Holland. Sitting in the
back was a thickset middle-aged man, wearing a broad-
rimmed black hat. Holland was pushed roughly inside
and another detective occupied the window seat, trap-
ping him in the middle. The car stank of sweat and stale
cigarettes.

The man in black punched Holland hard on the arm, as though he was being friendly, but the punch was meant to hurt. "You're full of tricks. Life's all bread and circuses for young boyos like you, isn't it?"

Holland didn't respond. The man smiled and punched him on the same spot just as hard. Pain blossomed out from Holland's muscles. It felt as if he were shattering the surface of the bone. "Amn't I right?" the man asked.

Holland's head fell forward and the man in the black hat seemed satisfied.

"The Castle," he ordered. "We'll open up your *béal* for you."

He was driven to the intelligence department of Dublin Castle and shown into a room where two young men were sprawled out on a couple of chairs. The walls were plastered with photographs of well-known Republicans.

Holland was told to sit down. He took out a cigarette and lit it. They asked him about Farkas, his clients, how he'd been recruited. Holland gave them as little information as he could. They threatened him but he found it hard to take them seriously. He knew one of them from his days as a volunteer in the Movement. After a while they simply gave up. A man came in and they were all handed cups of tea.

"What's this all about?" Holland asked innocently. "Has Mr Farkas been arrested or something?"

The two men glanced at each other.

"There's no harm in telling him," said one of them. The other man looked at Holland.

"Your employer's disappeared. Neighbours reported armed men going through his house. And then we discover that a notorious Republican is working for him. Suspicious?"

"As the lawyers would say, it's all circumstantial," said Holland.

"I'm afraid we'll have to let the other lads have you," said the other Branch man. "Are you sure there's nothing else you can tell us?"

Holland shrugged.

They looked apologetic, like schoolboys forced to send one of their comrades to a caning. Then the Guards came for him. He was taken in a car to the Bridewell and immediately brought to an interrogation room. By this time he was groggy and weak from hunger. Two men kept at him for four hours straight and then two more started to work on him. It was easy not to tell them anything, even when they boxed him or threatened to break his neck. At the worst moments he imagined himself floating in space just below the ceiling, looking down upon them.

He knew little that could be useful to them. Although he had kept notes of Farkas' guests and their business, it never amounted to very much. With his rudimentary German, he had registered that funds were flowing from Germany to Sweden and Portugal and sometimes back again. In his weakened state, he felt he could see these rivers of money moving ceaselessly across the Continent obeying their own mysterious laws of flow and return. If he babbled some of this to his interrogators, it would have meant nothing to them. He told them freely all that they wanted to know about his job: none of this information was proscribed by oath. His innocence, his ignorance, became apparent even under the bluff of secrecy forced upon him by membership of the Movement. Finally, when they had worn themselves out, he was shown into a cold cell and given a mug of lukewarm tea and a plate of bread and margarine. There was a filthy blanket on the stained mattress. Even in a state of exhaustion, it made him smile: the blanket had the date 1911 on it, when the Brits were the ones doing the torturing.

12

They came when Sabine least expected it. She had gone out to buy milk and cheese at a corner shop during the afternoon and was away for no more than twenty minutes. She wasn't sure whether she had simply been lucky to be out when they had raided her flat or if they had waited until she had left before breaking in.

On her return from the shop, she caught sight of one of the intruders standing at her door. In the poor light offered by the feeble bulb above the entrance, he appeared oafish and enormous. His body was encased within a huge greatcoat and a trilby was pulled down over his forehead, keeping all but the tip of his nose in deep shadow. Despite his size, he moved rapidly up the steps and along the pavement with the air of a man who had been invited to a house and forced to stay too long.

Sabine had no desire to confront him. She had heard too much about visits like that in Germany. Instead she went directly up to Mrs Fitzgibbons' and rang the doorbell. Luckily her landlady was at home. She was ushered in and they both crept to the window to see what was happening. But the street was deserted. After half-an-hour Mrs Fitzgibbons decided that it was safe to check the flat, but she refused to allow Sabine accompany her. When she returned, she told Sabine that the lock had been smashed and that the place was in a shambles. Sabine's belongings were scattered all over the room but her most valuable possessions had not been touched. Mrs Fitzgibbons went back to gather up jewellery and a book of photographs and took them up to her own place for safekeeping.

The two women talked all through the evening, drinking coffee and later sherry, trying to decide what Sabine should do. Mrs Fitzgibbons had no great opinion of the police.

"They are in the hands of that brute O'Duffy. For all we know, it could have been the Special Branch who turned your flat upside down."

She suggested that the best course of action was for Sabine to leave the country: Mrs Fitzgibbons had a sister in London who could help. With her proficiency in European languages, Sabine would have no trouble finding secretarial work.

"Isn't there anyone who could help you now that your employer has gone away?"

Sabine shook her head.

"What about the young man who drove the car that evening? He seemed like a very nice young chap. He helped you out once before, didn't he? What did he call himself? What was it now? It didn't sound terribly Irish. His name reminded me of a place in Europe for some reason."

"Byrne."

"Oh yes," said Mrs Fitzgibbon distractedly, having had another name in her head.

Naming him forced Sabine to remember him. She had tried to humiliate Holland in every way she could think of, but he had never once reacted to her provocations. She did not want to involve him, but how else could she escape from this city? The railway stations would be watched. Her complexion was too dark for her to be taken for a local and her accent was more English than Irish. On her own, a single female, she wouldn't stand a chance. She hadn't told Mrs Fitzgibbons about her true status. Her visa had expired; she was an illegal alien. If she were caught, they would detain her. They might even send her back to Germany. The pressure of thinking about this, knowing that she would have to reach a decision, made Sabine feel ill. She found herself calling the number of Holland's lodgings. A woman picked up the phone and Sabine felt an instant urge to replace the receiver. But Mrs Fitzgibbons' soft blue eyes, her expectant half-smile, forced her to continue. She asked to speak to Tom Byrne. There was a long pause as if the lady at the other end needed time to consider this request.

"I'll find him for you," said Mrs Mullen finally.

Holland was lying asleep in bed when his landlady knocked on his door. He was still groggy after his day in detention and his body was covered in bruises. His ribs sent lightning rods of pain into his head as he bent over to pull on his trousers, and he idly wondered whether the Free Staters had broken any of them. Gripping the banisters, he came down the stairs and picked up the receiver.

Sabine's voice moved through his head like a warm swell, all physical pain momentarily forgotten. Her anxiety was obvious, however hard she tried to disguise it.

"Do you know that Farkas has disappeared?"

"Yes," said Holland. "Whatever you do, don't go to the office."

"I need to leave the country."

"I'll come round your place tomorrow, after dark."

By early morning the city streets were full of a thick, dank fog. In backyards and laneways it was so dense that even the outlines of the buildings disappeared. Sabine imagined armies of men in greatcoats restlessly pacing the street. She had stayed inside with Mrs Fitzgibbons all day: only once was she left alone, when her landlady ventured out to buy bread, milk and eggs for them in a local shop.

It was growing dark as Holland walked to the lock-up to pick up the car. The pain in his ribs had eased. He was carrying the Parabellum, a change of clothes and his shaving gear. When he got to the Wolseley, he checked the petrol, oil and water before driving to Rathmines. He parked the car in a side street a few hundred yards from the entrance to Sabine's street, and walked the rest of the way. Mrs Fitzgibbons met him at the door.

"Here's your knight on a white steed," she shouted. Sabine came out, smiled awkwardly, and thanked him for coming. She noticed but did not mention the bruising on Holland's face.

"I know you're not officially employed by the company any more," she said in a stilted voice, "but could you drive me to the mail boat for the night crossing?"

Holland said he would do whatever she wanted.

With Holland and Mrs Fitzgibbons watching the street, Sabine risked a trip down to her own flat. As Mrs Fitzgibbon had told her, the place had been turned upside down, but there was no indication that the intruders had broken the lock. She assumed that this was just another example of Irish hyperbole on the part of her landlady. Without turning on a light, she packed a suitcase with clothes, carefully stowing the few photographs she had brought from Berlin at the bottom. She allowed herself only three books.

Mrs Fitzgibbons prepared egg sandwiches and a flask of coffee for the journey. Before they left, the two women hugged each other, and Mrs Fitzgibbon wiped away the beginning of tears.

Holland drove towards the sea. The lonesome cries of the fog-signal booming across the bay seemed to be beckoning them.

Sabine was the first to speak. "You didn't say what happened in England."

"I'm not sure what happened myself. All I know is that I ended up in a shooting match with some of Farkas' acquaintances in a field."

"Who were they?"

"Farkas said they were German intelligence, but they seemed a bit amateurish. One of them had a funny medal round his neck."

"A swastika?"

"No like this." He drew a symbol on the condensation at the bottom of the windscreen. Sabine's body froze beside him.

"What is it?"

"Have you never seen a Star of David before?"

"They were Jews?"

"Zionists probably. Did you hit any of them?"

"I don't think so," Holland lied. "They just ran off. Does this mean that these Zionists are after us too? Why are they involved?"

Sabine smiled enigmatically. "I don't think anyone is after us. It's Farkas they want. He must have got—what do you say?—cold feet. He has access to all the clients' money and he has just disappeared."

They turned onto the coast road; there were streetlights on one side and the great black swell of the sea on the other.

Holland suddenly pulled into the kerb to stop. He turned to Sabine.

"I think we're walking into a trap. If they can't find Farkas, they'll come after you. There'll be someone at the pier or someone waiting for you on the boat."

Sabine just stared at him.

"It's your life. You have to make a decision."

"There's no proof. I don't have anything they want. All I wish to do *now* is to get away from this crazy island and go back to England."

"All right, I'll keep going. But if there's anything suspicious, we'll turn back. I'm not going to just hand you over to them."

"That's agreed. But if all is normal, I take the boat, yes?"

They drove in silence the rest of the way to Dun Laoghaire. As they approached the pier, Holland cut his lights and slowed the car to a crawl. His eyes ran along the line of waiting vehicles. Then he made a sudden u-turn, almost colliding with an oncoming delivery van, and sped away. He turned down two side streets and then parked. Sabine was close to tears.

"What was it? I want to go back."

"I saw the same car the night Farkas took us to the Shelbourne. A blue Packard, two men in it."

Sabine clenched her fists and had to stop herself banging them on the dashboard.

"You're making it up. I didn't see anything," she shrieked.

"They were there. It was the same car."

"What now?" she asked. "Can you take me back to Mrs Fitzgibbons?" All power over her destiny had deserted her. She could not think ahead. She had already imagined herself getting off the boat at Holyhead, sitting on the train as it pulled into Euston Station.

"Too late for that. We have to get out of Dublin, Sabine," said Holland, self-conscious about appropriating her name to make his point. "We can stay at my uncle's place. No one will find us there."

Holland did not drive directly out of the city. Now that it was night, the fog seemed even denser: it rose up like a wall before the searching headlights of the Wolseley. In the complex network of streets on the northside of the city, Holland kept pulling over and stopping the engine in order to check if they were being followed, even though he knew that tailing a car through the foggy streets would be extremely difficult.

To Sabine, Dublin was a labyrinth, identical streets looming up like fake screens, blocking off every advance. The dark fug inside the car, the smell of leather and tobacco made her feel ill. After an hour she noticed that they were driving along open roads with the grainy images of fields and hedgerows on either side. The fog dissipated, and what light remained was embedded in the distance, faint flickerings in a sea of darkness.

"Where are we now?" she asked, drawing her arms tight around herself.

"County Meath. Heading towards Kells."

The names meant nothing to her, but she noted the small towns they were driving through. Their empty streets reminded her of open-air stages awaiting actors and music. She saw churches perched on hills, churches of grey granite which looked more like miniature castles than places of worship.

After Kells, the road began to climb and the overhanging trees formed an arch above their heads as though they were travelling through a vast tunnel. Sabine felt she was entering another kind of Ireland, the Ireland that lived beyond the gravitational pull of Dublin.

Although she had spent nearly five months in the country, Sabine had never been farther than the mountains of Wicklow. On the maps she had seen, the hinterland appeared to be as featureless as the ocean, with only a few tiny towns scattered like buoys to break up the monotony. In Germany, Sabine had always been too scared to explore the countryside. In her imagination, it was full of peasants in folk costumes and marching, uniformed youth. All her concepts of rural life came from her mother, who had spent most of her childhood in Poland. But even this experience was regarded as a joke in the family. Her mother's true life had not begun until her family had taken her to Berlin, where she had been introduced to her husband. He, by contrast, was the pure urbanite, unsullied by rural experiences: he was *Herr Doktor*, an educated modern man and he had claimed Sabine's mother as if she were a patch of uncultivated land.

The bleakness of the journey made Sabine feel like talking. Like so many men, Holland seemed perfectly happy wrapped inside a brooding silence. She wanted to be strong, but she needed the comfort of words.

"Do you know," she began, "the Romans would have written *hic sunt leones* about this place? That's what they put on the maps of the lands west of the Danube."

"Latin, is it?"

"It means 'here are lions'."

Holland smiled: "You'll get on well with my uncle. He speaks the old Latin too. Very well-read man."

"Is he a farmer?" Sabine recalled reading that most Irish people were farmers.

"He gets a pension."

Their headlights burned through the deep green foliage. The rest of the countryside fell away into a monotonous blackness. Even the distant lights grew fewer and fewer as though civilization itself was being extinguished around them. Sabine's head felt heavy and she began to doze. She was back in her parents' home in

Dragonerstrasse, Berlin, the flat her parents were forced to move to when they lost their city-centre clinic. They were sitting around the kitchen table, arguing and joking. Her father beckoned to her as though to impart some important message. She made out the first few words and then another voice broke in. Holland was shaking her by the shoulder. Sabine crawled out of her dream and looked out the window. At first she saw nothing; then gradually her eyes adjusted and she realised that Holland had stopped the car on the crest of a hill. Far below them, the dawn was beginning to creep over a vast swathe of fields and woods. Coils of grey mist snaked between the trees and hedges. The shock of waking from the familiarities of Berlin to this panorama in the cold centre of an alien island was too much for her. Tears clouded her sight. Sobs shook her chest and she felt like calling out the names of her parents, shouting them out to the empty nameless countryside. She covered her eyes with her hands.

Holland frowned and continued to watch the sunlight move across the fields.

"So much for the lovely magic of the dawn," he said.

Before restarting the car, he handed her a paper handkerchief from the supply Farkas had bought for the glove compartment. They drove on for a while in silence, heading continuously downhill towards the town of Oldcastle.

"Come on, talk to me. If you won't let me smoke, help me stay awake at least." He opened his window and the car filled up with raw freezing air. "Breathe that in. It will do you good."

"I'm sorry about my behaviour. I just was overcome. I thought of my family and friends in Germany. I know I cannot go back. The last news is worse and worse."

"Well, at least you're talking. Talking is the best medicine. That's what my mother always used to say."

"But your friend the Republican would say something else—that a bullet was the best medicine."

The old Sabine is back, thought Holland.

"That's just an historical thing. The Irish did an awful lot of talking and they didn't get anywhere. It was only when they took up the gun that the English paid attention. As our Mr McGuire used to say: 'Real politics comes from the front end of a revolver. All the rest is just exercise for the jaws.'"

"I'll talk to you if you'll please shut that window."

"Anything for the lady." Holland wound up the window and nearly crashed the car while negotiating a sharp bend at the same time.

"Why are there those black marks on your face?"

"A misunderstanding between me and the civic guards. They locked me up for a few hours after Farkas disappeared. And, as you can see, they weren't very civic." There was no sign that Sabine had understood the pun. Holland changed tack: "By the way, what do you think has happened to our old boss?"

"Perhaps they have—what do you say?—captured him. I have no idea; it all just makes me frightened."

"A smart fella like Farkas; he must have had an escape plan. I can't believe they just came out to his house and grabbed him, whoever they were."

"I feared they would come after me as well."

She looked as if she was going to cry again.

"Don't worry. You'll be safe where I'm taking you."

"Where is this place? The landscape here is so melancholic."

"Melancholic?"

"The emptiness; all the ruins. There is something sad about the sky, the light."

The truth was that even the lived-in houses appeared grim to Sabine. She had expected rural Ireland to be full of life and colour, like the place their leader de Valera described on the wireless. Instead of bright homesteads with thatched roofs and timber frames, she saw only the occasional ugly brick or grey stone house, angrily dominating a hill or guarding a stand of trees.

"You should see the West of Ireland. That's really sad. There are whole villages deserted, ruined castles. It's like something sucked all the people out of the place."

"When were you in the West?"

"I was sent there … a while back."

"A secret mission?"

"Yes, a secret mission. For training purposes." Holland realised he was telling her too much and cut himself off. He began to hum.

They entered Oldcastle. Because it was so early, the streets were deserted. The dull houses, with their white lace curtains and poorly painted doors, stared menacingly at them. Holland stopped in the square. Roads led off in different directions. He couldn't remember which one to take.

"You've got to let me have one cigarette, Sabine. I can't think without one."

Sabine opened the window on her side and Holland lit up.

"Better, better," he muttered. He squinted at one of the signs. "Well, we don't want to go to Ballyjamesduff, that's for sure. Wait a second! Castlepollard must be down that road on the left. That means we need to go straight up that way there."

Holland shifted into first gear and they drove past a hotel and bank and then took a left. The countryside surrounded them once more and they retreated into their separate silences. For what seemed an eternity to Sabine they negotiated a series of hill and bends Holland took a last savage drag on his cigarette, wound down the window and tossed out the butt. "How long were you in London?"

"Long enough to know I did not like it. It's similar to Berlin only bigger. Everyone is in a ghetto of some kind—the Irish, the Italians, the Jews. Even the English are in their class ghettos."

"Well, as you know, I've only been there once. And that was not a big success. I'm a country boy at heart."

Holland remembered the flat field and how lucky he was to have escaped alive. He laughed; he was so tired that the interior of the car was beginning to blur and only the hedgerows outside were in focus. So far though, everything was going according to plan. Now that they were spinning through the gentle hilly landscape west of Oldcastle, he even felt at ease. The world of the city, its streets hanging in his mind like grey strips of film full of discordant pictures, was behind him. He could sense calm and well-being radiating from the vast green warmth of the Irish interior.

They drove through an undulating landscape with beech trees on either side of the road and a large lake that shimmered seductively on their left. Sometimes the lake was close to them and sometimes distant. Occasionally it disappeared behind walls of vegetation. In the fields adjoining the lake, ring forts speckled the landscape like giant fungal growths. Holland whistled happily to himself. The car lurched around corners as his reactions became duller: luckily there was still no traffic on the road.

Sabine was worried that his concentration would fail them, but she could do nothing: she had never learnt to drive. They approached a particularly sharp right bend, heavy foliage and trees blocking their view of the road rising ahead. Instead of turning with the road, Holland swerved sharply into what seemed to Sabine to be a wall of greenery. She let out a screech and raised her hands to cover her face. The car was airborne for an instant, and then landed with a jarring thud as they drove directly through what looked like a door in the hedgerow and reappeared on a narrow lane on the other side.

Holland laughed: "Sorry, I didn't mean to frighten you. I have to find a place to hide the car."

Sabine felt ashamed that she could be so easily tricked.

Holland pitched the car to the left, changed down to first gear and drove along a muddy track with bogland on either side. The track was pitted with deep trenches filled with water, and the Wolseley rose and fell like a ship in heavy seas. Holland pulled into a clearing at the edge of the bog and parked the car on the grass behind a stand of birch trees.

He looked at his watch. It was 6.30 in the morning.

"What do we do now?" Sabine asked.

"We'll leave the car here, and walk to Finea."

"Won't anyone see it?"

"No one ever comes down this way."

They both got out. It was strange for Sabine to find herself in the middle of this alien countryside. While on the move, none of it had seemed quite real, but now there was no escaping the melancholy impression it made upon her. In Germany the countryside was orderly, composed of sections of forest and fields, with houses and farms dotted equidistant from each other. By comparison, the Irish landscape was chaotic and incoherent. Even the roads seemed to wander randomly in every direction.

Holland broke off branches and foliage to cover the outline of the car, while Sabine looked around. The bog was a tangle of discordant colours, purples merging into acidic greens and yellows; the lake, with its turbulent grey waves, seemed frighteningly divorced from the world of human beings; the hillside fields she could spy in the distance were empty and of little obvious purpose to man or beast.

Holland collected their luggage from the boot and they walked back towards the boreen they had entered so abruptly. They turned left and finished the rest of their sandwiches as they walked. On one side, the bog, which was higher than the level of the road, was spiked with rusting bedsteads and the remains of an old model T-Ford. There was even a chimney top. Holland fooled Sabine into believing that the bog had swallowed up an entire Irish village, suffocating the inhabitants in their beds.

After about fifteen minutes, they came to a crude junction. Holland's senses sharpened because he knew there was a police barracks about twenty yards to their right.

"There's a song about this place, but I'll tell you about it another time."

Sabine stayed with their luggage while Holland investigated the road. There was no traffic and no sign of human activity around the barracks. They crossed the steep-backed bridge to enter the deserted main street of the village, and then walked along a path skirting the bridge down to the river.

Holland picked out a boat with the name *Pan Glas* written in Celtic script on the gunwale.

He looked at Sabine. "Only my Uncle FX would choose a name like that for a boat."

He stowed their luggage in the back and arranged the oars.

Sabine, exhausted and cranky, looked at him incredulously: "You do not expect me to get in to that?"

He did and she felt a sickness of unease grip her stomach as she swayed and balanced at the end of the boat. Holland just laughed and set his hands to the oars. The water looked treacherously deep and black to her. Once Holland had pushed off, she felt the current grip them like a giant hand and sweep the boat into the dull green frontier of trees and fields. She was so tired and out of sorts that even German words abandoned her. Holland sensed her predicament and talked soothingly to her as though she were a child. He told her the river would take them to another lake, and that his uncle lived on the far shore of that lake. The river, though, went on and on, he said in a low gentle voice, all the way to the mighty Shannon and eventually the sea. Sabine hardly listened; her hands grasped the gunwales as though her life depended on it.

The village with the barracks perched over the bridge soon disappeared from view, much to Holland's relief. Sand martins and house martins chattered and scoured the air for insects. A heron eyed them cautiously as it stalked the riverbank and then flew away with slow, ponderous beats of its wings. They floated past the reed beds and sedges that grew thickly where the river met the lake until their boat, as though attracted by a powerful magnet, was suddenly drawn into the open waters of Lough Kinale.

A nameless fear gripped Sabine when the boat began to lurch and sway under the influence of the waves on the lake surface: she feared that she was vanishing into a cold jungle from which she would never return.

Holland now began to row in earnest, against the wind from the south and the choppy waters. They followed a deserted shoreline, littered with boulders and spume that looked like snow from a distance, then rowed past the mouth of another river and circled a headland flanked by impenetrable reed beds with a ring fort in the middle. Small rafts of ducks bobbed on the grey water. Holland kept as far away from them as he could: he did not want to raise them and so draw attention to the boat.

"Are you sure you know where he lives?" Sabine asked. Besides a few grey shapes on the distant hills, she had yet to see a single house.

"He lives on the Abbeylara side," Holland shouted through the wind.

"And you said his name was Max or Rex?"

"No, FX, short for Francis Xavier. My grandmother was a very pious woman, and she wanted him to join the priesthood. But he couldn't take it, and ended up coming back here."

They gradually made their way over to the thickly wooded far shore. Holland beached the boat and tied it to a rock. Sabine stood up and Holland caught hold of her to help her out. He admired her body, so slim, taut and elegant.

Her impression of him was that he was as solid and substantial as the rocks along the shore. By comparison, her own body was paper-light and adrift.

They trudged along a tiny path, dragging their luggage, Sabine close to exhaustion. Holland was in better spirits, although his arms were aching from the effort of driving so far and then vigorously rowing. On the other side of a thicket of brambles and blackthorn bushes, they came upon a rundown two-storey house. There was no sign of life. They dropped their bags and Holland peered through the kitchen window.

"Do you think he still lives here?" Sabine asked.

"He's probably in the bed. It's still very early. I'll give a knock at the door."

An upstairs window was suddenly heaved up and a dishevelled grey head shot out.

"What the—! Is that you, Orwen? My God, what time is it? Wait there; I'll be down in a tick."

"Orwen!" exclaimed Sabine. "*That's* your name?"

Holland rubbed his forehead.

"I prefer to be called Holland," he said without thinking.

The door opened and they were ushered inside. FX wore an old coat over his pyjamas. He was a wiry little man in his mid-fifties.

"You have a young lady with you. What next! The poor girl must be cold; that's a fresh wind from the lake. Come in and I'll stick a few bits of turf on the fire."

FX showed them into a large kitchen, which also served as living room and dining room. The room was dark and untidy; ancient wallpaper, stained and brown, covered the walls. To Sabine the house and its furnishings appeared to have remained unchanged since the middle of the nineteenth century: the only exception was a large upright wireless set on a wooden table beside the fire. For a second, she stood mesmerised by the numbers on the white dial, imagining tuning into the voices of her home city in Germany.

Holland and his uncle talked about old times. When the fire was lit, FX put on a kettle for tea. For the first time since their flight from Dublin, time expanded for Sabine and Holland. FX began to ask why they were visiting.

Holland said: "I have to ask you a favour. We need you to put us up for a while, and keep it quiet. It doesn't matter so much if the neighbours know that I'm here but they mustn't see Sabine."

"Ah, Sabine, what a wonderful name! Like the ancient Sabeans. You must be French."

Sabine ought to have said German, even though she knew she no longer was considered a German. Instead she said: "I'm a Jew."

FX's eyes opened slightly wider.

"A Jew," he repeated delicately as if testing the word on his tongue. "A Jew, imagine that."

Sabine noticed that FX's face flushed. Here too, she thought; here too, they despise us.

"A very fine people, the Jews. Do you speak Hebrew at all? I have tried to learn a little from a book by a scholar from Trinity College, but I'm finding it very difficult. The vowels, you see, are hard to make out."

Sabine had to confess that she knew only a few words of Hebrew, and could not read the language at all.

"A pity. The Latin is so much easier. *Merses profundo: pulchrior evenit.* I'm reading Horace again." Sabine tried to look interested. FX glanced up at Holland. "Is this the reason for your escape, because your friend here is Jewish? I thought the fascists were beat?"

"It's like this, FX. Sabine and I work in the same company and now our boss has disappeared. A lot of people really want to get hold of him. They seem to think Sabine knows where he is and they're prepared to kill. I can testify to that. They've already ransacked her flat in Dublin. She is not even sure she'd be safe in England. In any case, I thought she could lie low for a week or so and then try to get the ferry from Derry to Glasgow. No one would expect her to head that way."

"And the police?"

"Well, you know what they're like: they see Republican involvement everywhere. They picked me up and bashed me around for information. Excuse the language, but they're a bunch of bloody thugs."

His uncle closed his eyes and joined the tips of his fingers.

"I see, I see," he said at last, although Sabine was not sure what it was exactly that he had understood.

"Is it all right if we stay with you?"

"Yes, yes, of course."

Holland sensed reluctance.

"Will this cause any problems?"

FX glanced at Sabine. His grey eyes seemed unusually bright, like a bird's.

"It's not the local guards," he intoned slowly. "They're buffoons. They know nothing and they're interested in less. The problem is … elsewhere."

He uttered the last sentence so quietly that Sabine thought he had not meant her to hear it. He continued: "The parish priest you see… he's very intemperate regarding some matters…."

"What do you mean?" Holland said.

FX cleared his throat and looked once more at Sabine. This time their eyes met. He was addressing her rather than Holland.

"Well, you get this group of young lads and you offer the quickest of them an education which they would otherwise never get. You lock them in a seminary with a bunch of other young fellows and you fill up their heads with Latin and Greek. You cut them off from womenfolk. They hardly see a female of their own age from one month to the other. And after years of this, the result turns out to be something like our Father Carney. He's obsessed with what he likes to call depravity and 'occasions of sin', although I doubt very much he has a clear idea of what they are. All I know is that he's going to smell some depravity and occasions of sin around here unless we think of something."

"I don't understand," said Sabine, "You're frightened of what the local Catholic priest thinks? You need not worry. Holland and myself – we are not lovers."

FX laughed. His laughter was surprisingly youthful, as though Sabine had awakened it from some deep cellar in his past. "I'm afraid that argument won't cut any ice with Father Carney. His mind sees only the one sin. He'd rather see murderers walk the streets than any sugges-tion of moral laxity. And you being a foreigner too: he'll expect the very worst."

"Nobody saw us arrive," Holland said practically. "We'll just have to keep Sabine out of the way for the time being."

"We'll see how things go."

Sabine felt that she had travelled from the insanity of her own country only to be locked away in the grim madness of another.

13

FX prepared a breakfast of rashers and eggs. He cut the bacon himself, thick and fat, from a salted pig hanging in the hallway. There was also homemade soda bread and cups of chestnut brown tea; and the evening ended with exactly the same meal. While FX was pottering about outside, Sabine looked squarely at Holland and told him that she couldn't go on eating like this. Sabine did not eat pig meat if she could avoid it, not because she was Jewish, she told him, but because the taste of it made her nauseous.

Holland felt ashamed on his uncle's behalf. He searched through his pockets, unwrapping the various balls of notes and counting the coins. His savings amounted to about £15, enough to allow them to eat well for a considerable period.

"I'll go and have a word with him," he said.

He found FX repairing a door on one of the outhouses. While he hammered away, Holland talked to him about the weather before getting to the point.

"You know, FX, we're well able to pay our way. For food and that."

He gave the word "we" a strong emphasis, which FX duly noticed.

"We, we… that girl will soon be twisting you around her little finger." He stood up to laugh.

Holland felt foolish. "We can pay for the food we eat. I'll pay for it."

His words sounded ungrateful, but FX's face just crumpled up into a far-away smile.

"No, no, I won't hear of it. You're my guests. There's plenty of food in this house. I have potatoes and vegetables in the garden. The neighbours are very good to me. They often come by with part of a beast or a dozen eggs."

Holland saw his chance: "That could be a problem for us if they're dropping in all the time. It'll be hard to keep Sabine out of the way, do you see?"

FX abruptly stopped working and stared at Holland.

"There's another thing I've been meaning to say. You know I've taken Dev's pension. That mean's I've agreed that the war's over. I can't have you here if—"

"If I'm still in the Movement? No, it's all over as far as I'm concerned."

FX smiled, this time intensely. "After I'm gone, this'll be your place. It's not much, but it is land. And there's the lake. Maybe the English will start coming back to fish. All I know is that it won't do you much good if you're rotting in jail or on the run."

"I'm out of it. Scout's honour."

"You were never in the scouts."

The two men eyed each other as though suddenly conscious of a boundary between them.

FX put down his hammer and took hold of Holland's arm. "Come with me. I might have a way to keep your ladyfriend out of sight."

It was late in the evening and the temperature was pleasant if cooler than Sabine would have expected for the time of year. She was well rested: during the afternoon she had fallen asleep on the leather sofa in the front room. Holland had covered her with a blanket and she had got at least three hours' sleep. When she awoke, she was disorientated, as though her internal compass was spinning wildly out of control. Instead of evening time, it was morning and, instead of west, she found herself in the east, in Poland. Holland walked in and she babbled to him in a mixture of Yiddish and Polish.

To his credit he made no comment, just handed her a cup of dark tea. Her bewilderment subsided. She realised that the vast greenness outside was not part of the Continent; that there was a lake and house and two men in a world of English speakers.

After she had finished her tea, Holland asked if she felt like walking. They strolled out through the trees at the back of the house and began to follow the same path they had taken that morning.

"Where are you leading me?" Sabine asked in mock suspicion.

"You'll see."

Farther along the shore they could hear noises—scraping sounds like something sharp being dragged across a wooden floor. The sounds were coming from behind a mixed copse of birch and ash trees. Sabine became anxious, but Holland just smiled and insisted that she follow him into the trees. To her surprise, she found herself in front of a tiny cottage built of dressed stone. FX emerged from the inside and stood at the door to usher them in. There were only two rooms, a kitchen and a tiny bedroom. The interior was very dusty, but despite the cottage's proximity to the lake, there was no hint of dampness.

FX showed them around as though they he were an estate agent and they a newly wed couple, in need of accommodation.

"We used to rent it out to fishermen, wealthy English gentlemen for the most part. That was before the Troubles. The roof is sound. They really knew how to build things to last in those days. There's no running water or gas or anything, but there's a pump out the back and a sort of outdoor lavatory. I can supply you with a bed and a few sticks of furniture."

"And a lamp?" Holland asked.

"Oh yes, of course."

Up until now, Sabine had not spoken. She felt the gloominess of the encroaching trees and the pagan aura of the lake. Her heart fluttered as she tried to manage her fear. She could imagine what the cottage would be like at night, abandoned, without a single light anywhere, and only the wild birds and her imagination to keep her company.

"I don't think I can stay here," she said slowly.

FX misunderstood her and smiled broadly. "Oh I know it looks a mess now but we'll fix the place up, clean it out. It'll be as clean as the inside of a churn when we're finished with it."

Holland cleared his throat and said: "I can come down and keep you company. You'll be safe here. It's just until we figure out what to do next."

Sabine spent that night huddled in a ball in the spare bedroom of FX's house. The room smelt of mothballs and damp wood and was bitterly cold. The floorboards creaked at irregular intervals and she thought of Holland's dead mother, whom the two men had spoken of that night by the fire. Holland took the couch in the front room. It was far too small for him, but he too finally slept.

The next morning the two men borrowed an extra bike from a neighbouring farm and cycled in to Abbeylara, the nearest village, to buy groceries.

They arranged their bicycles beside the wall of the only grocery shop and pub. Before going inside, FX warned Holland about the owner, a retired policeman, but told him that it was usually his wife who served in the shop. Holland decided to take the chance: there was nothing more suspicious than acting as though one had something to hide. Inside, a gangly woman in her fifties stood behind the wooden counter. She smiled at FX and examined Holland with great interest.

"So someone got the looks in your family," she said.

FX laughed. "You'll be trying to recruit him for the local dances now I suppose."

"Ah, most of the young wans have gone—to Dublin or to England."

They bought flour, cheese, butter and tinned vegetables, as well as some cakes which Holland thought Sabine might like.

On the way back, FX punched him on the arm and told him that his mother shouldn't have fed him so well.

"I have my size from my father," Holland said truculently.

"He was a good enough man in his own way, but may hell's fire take the rest of that family. And I do mean that!"

After they had returned and eaten lunch, the two men began to move furniture down to the cottage. They then built a stack of turf at the gable end and covered it with a sheet of tarpaulin. Sabine put on her oldest clothes to sweep and wash the floors: in the kitchen she scoured any surface she could reach. Holland 'skited some soapy water on the windows and wiped them until they shone.

Sabine made them some dinner from the tinned vegetables and boiled potatoes. When they had finished eating, and the two men began to do the washing up, she felt the need to be alone. She walked down to the water's edge and sat herself on a flat-topped rock. The stone felt pleasant and cool, the waters lapped gently against the foreshore. Shadows hung from the bushes and trees, and tiny waves washed over a world of darkness under the lake. There was barely a breath of wind. Tufted ducks rose with difficulty from the surface as though the water was covered in a sheen of oil. Sabine could imagine the old gods of the Irish lurking in the shadows and among the strangely shaped stones.

An incandescent moon, almost perfectly round, moved over the lake, floating in a sky that remained unnaturally bright. She was reminded of her mother's stories about the white nights of the Russian summer. And like her image of Russia, where she had never been, the landscape here struck her as ancient and primitive. She felt she had been removed to another era, where time was circular and the evolution of machines and a modern society had yet to take place. Here there were only the old standbys of all human cultures: the unseeing face of the moon over the land, the naked power of the seasons and the growth of plants.

She was still enraptured by these thoughts of the distant past when she heard a noise behind her. It was Holland: she was surprised how close he had come to her without her noticing. Like a cat.

"Did I frighten you?"

She shook her head.

"I've grown used to you."

Holland laughed. "Always the put-down. I suppose you still think of me as a savage?"

It was an unusually bold speech. Holland had never asked for her opinion before. He stood waiting for her reply and she could see he was ill at ease. She liked him then, his boyishness. This image contrasted with the other more jarring pictures she had of him, carelessly driving the car, holding a gun, and punching the fascist on Rathmines Road.

"You're not a savage, you're a *Knabe*."

"A what?"

Sabine gave him an impish smile. "It's the German word for a lad."

"There you are, making fun of me again," said Holland, smiling. He sat down on the rock adjoining hers. It was uncomfortably sharp and pitted, but he managed to find some purchase on it.

Holland said: "It's strange here. I remember the nights were always as black as tar. You could almost touch it, it was so dark. But just look at the sky tonight."

"Were you brought up in the country?"

"When I was small, yes. Then I went to Dublin with my mother."

"And you came here for holidays?"

"I wouldn't call them holidays exactly. We never had enough money for that. We would come down for a week or two and live off my uncle. He had a few cows at the time. I'd help him out. He tried to teach me Greek and Latin when I was milking them: that wasn't so much fun."

"You've no brothers or sisters?"

"No. Besides FX, I don't have anybody—a strange situation to be in. But you haven't told me anything about yourself."

Sabine was suddenly defensive. Her black eyes ranged over the darkening landscape. "I don't want to talk about Germany, Holland."

"You'd prefer to talk about Holland than Germany?"

Her lips made an attempt at a smile. She gave Holland a sceptical look.

"Tell me how you got involved with the Republicans? That is interesting."

"I joined the Fianna when I was a boy."

"The what?"

"It's like the boy scouts, only more militant: it's called after an army they used to have in Ireland hundreds of years ago, to keep the foreigners out."

Sabine's eyes narrowed: "What did you do in this Fianna?"

"We marched a lot, sang nationalist songs, learnt Irish and history. Played sports, Irish sports of course—hurling and Gaelic football. We even went camping a few times, and got to handle guns."

Sabine looked more and more aghast, and Holland didn't understand why. Only West Brits had anything against the Fianna, he thought.

She looked at him angrily. "I suppose you beat up foreigners and threw bricks through shopkeepers' windows? Or all those without real Irish names."

"I think you've got the wrong end of the stick. We didn't do any of those things. We were very idealistic. That was where I met Caffrey."

"Who's Caffrey?"

Holland had made a gaffe: under normal circumstances, he would never have named his best friend to someone outside the Movement. But somehow it was natural to speak candidly to Sabine. She too was on the run and a foreigner—in Irish terms, a non-person.

"I introduced him as Byrne when we were in Bewley's. He has fair hair."

"The one who looks like a Nazi?"

"I wouldn't know; I've never met a Nazi."

Sabine felt she had gone too far. "I'm sorry for what I said. I don't mean it. I was thinking of my family in Germany when you came down here. Perhaps it is good for me to think of other things. But I cannot help comparing what I hear in Ireland with what I left in Germany. You can have no idea how bad it is there."

"You can talk to me about it if you like."

"You would not understand. I'm frightened about what has happened to my father and mother, and my brother. I haven't heard anything from them for weeks."

"What about Farkas? Was he not able to help you?"

"He tried, but even for him the situation was getting more difficult each day. And now he's gone too."

Holland thought he saw tears in Sabine's eyes. She turned away from him. "Tell me," she said, "was Caffrey the one you saved when you got that scar?"

"Yes. It happened because he couldn't resist making one of his usual smart-aleck comments."

Holland ran his finger along the outline of the cut and smiled to himself. He didn't look as if he would continue with the story.

"What happened to the man who did it? Did you shoot him?"

"Oh him; he ended up in hospital with a broken jaw. The funny thing was, Caffrey got off without a scratch. He's the luckiest bastard you ever met. Up he gets afterwards, shakes off the dust and says: 'Thank you very much, Holland. That's one for the book.' And the next thing he's off to meet some little mot at Nelson's Pillar. I'm hauled off to the doctor, bleeding like a pig of course."

"You must like him a lot?"

"I'm just used to him, I suppose. I've heard so many of his stories, sometimes I get mixed up about whether it was me or him they happened to. I even started to believe that I was born in Dublin and not down the country just because he was."

It was now Sabine's turn to be silent. Holland felt that he had spoken too much. He thought himself a poor storyteller, but it had looked like she was genuinely interested.

Sabine's eyes were rimmed by the remaining light in the sky. She leaned forward, towards him. In the twilight everything seemed evanescent except her eyes.

"You still haven't told me why you're involved, why you're risking your life for this organisation."

Holland gave her the usual spiel about Ireland's wrongs and England's iniquity; most of it regurgitated snippets from McDaid's outpourings. He mentioned invasions, the Famine, uprisings, massacres and Easter 1916 when a thousand rebels kept the British Empire at bay for nearly a week.

Sabine listened politely until he had finished.

"That's not a reason for becoming politically involved. Were any of your relatives killed in these risings?"

Holland shook his head. He didn't quite know what Sabine was getting at: all he knew was that he found her delving uncomfortable.

"You don't want to talk about Germany; well I don't really want to talk about this." His shoulders slumped; he rubbed his hands along his thighs and knees. "This is the way things are in this country. We've lived with this oppression for hundreds of years. And it is still going on. The English still run the country."

"Give me an example," said Sabine provocatively. "I haven't seen this oppression."

"You don't *see* it. It's just there, under the surface." Holland ran his hand through his hair. "I'll give you an example? Take any of the big firms in Dublin. Most of them are owned by Protestants, Unionists. They have pictures of the king on the wall and souvenirs from the time Queen Victoria visited the country. In all these firms you have a ceiling: no Catholic can advance any further than, say, senior clerk. That's the way it is and that's the way it's always been. It doesn't matter how good they are or how bad the Protestant clerks are. It's like a law of nature. Caffrey; he knew all about it. They fired him because he kicked up a fuss when they promoted some wall-eyed Protestant half-wit instead of him."

Sabine looked over the lake: "I see what you mean. So that is why your friend joined the rebels."

"No, you don't see anything. He was in the Movement before he got fired. He's always been in the Movement. Same as me."

Holland had become more heated than he'd intended. He wanted desperately to be able to hold a normal conversation with Sabine, but their minds seemed to be incompatible, as though they had been wired up differently.

Sabine got up and began to move back to the house. "I must go and sleep," she said.

"I was going to ask you about Farkas, and who's after him."

"We can talk in the morning."

"Are you going to sleep in the cottage? The bed's been set up."

Sabine moved away from him and into the darkness of the path. "I think I'll stay in the house again. I have to wash the sheets. Perhaps tomorrow."

The shape of her body merged into the dappled greys of the trees. The lake was now lighter than the shore and the sky lighter than the lake. Because it was midsummer, the night did not gather momentum from the sky, as one might have expected, but seemed to emerge slowly from the land. Darkness moved in the hollows and covered places and crept out from the stands of trees around the lake, and then finally, very slowly, began to seep upwards to fill the still radiant skies. It was only when the sky itself began to darken that Holland picked himself up and went back to the house.

14

The following day, after breakfast, Holland took FX's bike out of the outhouse and strapped a fishing rod to the bar. He packed a billhook and some sandwiches in his haversack.

He didn't tell Sabine where he was going. She still seemed to be annoyed with him; either that or she was indifferent to his activities. After finishing a bowl of porridge, she walked down to the cottage by the lake without saying a word, taking one of her books with her.

Once he'd adjusted the saddle, Holland set off. The bike needed oil but was otherwise in good condition. The weather was fine. Fluffy clouds filled the skies and it was hard to believe that there could be any danger in such a landscape. Everything in it, even the sky that enclosed it, was round, soft and unthreatening. He cycled through Abbeylara and turned right for Finea. After about half-an-hour the sweat had half blinded him and it felt as if an iron hoop had been inserted around his lungs. The constant hills wore him down; he was out of condition, unused to cycling more than few hundred yards at a time. When he approached Finea, he took a breather within sight of the barracks. Besides a squiggle of grey smoke hovering over the chimney, there was no sign of life from the local constabulary. The village seemed very quiet. He could make out a single car, an old jalopy with some fishing gear in the back, and a couple of drays. He mounted the bike again, passed the barracks, and turned left down the bog road he and Sabine had taken to reach Finea.

The Wolseley was where he'd left it. Apart from some bird droppings on the windows, and muck from the lane, it still looked like a new city car. He started the engine to make sure it was running properly. Then he switched it off and began to cut down branches and reeds with the billhook to add to the layer of camouflage that already covered it.

When he had finished, he walked down to the water's edge. Lough Sheelin looked vast. To the left there was a tiny sandy beach and in the distance an archipelago of small, densely wooded islands. A thin mist hung over the lake and the islands appeared to float over the surface as if anchored there by magnetism.

He remembered, when he was about ten or eleven, asking FX if this were the sea. His mother had laughed, displaying her fine white teeth.

For some reason this made him think of Sabine. He toyed vaguely with the idea of returning to Dublin and telling McDaid where she was. It would of course allow him to wash his hands of her and Farkas and start over. All that was required of him was to jump in the car and drive to Dublin: he could be there by the afternoon. Any Volunteer in the Movement would have done as much.

A vision of Sabine's bitter black eyes struck him. He tried to see her as a witch, making use of him, a little black Jewish hobgoblin. Her face became ugly and repugnant. He did his best to imagine what McDaid would have told him to do: he even tried to follow Caffrey's probable line of reasoning on the matter. Caffrey would have smirked and said: 'There's plenty of fish in the sea, old man.'

'All you have to do is get into the car,' he told himself. But he didn't move.

The tiny waves from the miniature sea lapped against the Lilliputian strand, mocking his attempts to think. It made him recall the sensation of lifting Sabine out of the boat when they arrived at the far side of the Lough Kinale. He remembered the comforting weight of her body, her trust in him.

Deep inside he knew he could not go against his own nature, his own feelings for her. He could not bear the thought of Sabine—who had escaped torture and death in Germany—facing the same treatment in Ireland. He threw a stone into the lake in a high long arc. It hit the water with a distinct 'plop', like a surprised human voice, before vanishing beneath the surface.

15

On 1 July 1937, the Free State voted for both the new constitution and a new government. Holland did not care much for either but used the occasion to take the train to Dublin. He knew there would be so many people milling about even in the small towns, people who normally wouldn't be seen from one end of the year to the other, that no one would notice an additional strange face.

The train arrived in Dublin during the afternoon and Holland found himself walking toward his old haunts. He had missed the place. He had even missed the smells of Stoneybatter: the stench of thousands of cattle pressed close together—soon to go to their deaths in English cities—the raw stink of pigsties hidden away in backstreets, the pungent aroma of hops and barley emanating from Jameson's distillery and the Guinness brewery.

Although he knew it was risky, he decided to visit his old digs to see if there were any messages for him, and to collect the allowance from his father's family which he hoped was still being sent there. Mrs Mullen was overwrought when she saw him. She pulled him into the kitchen and flung her arms around him.

"We all thought you were dead," she said. "I've rented out your room; you didn't let us know where you were. No one told me anything!"

Holland's feelings for Mrs Mullen were confused, but his main reaction at this moment was embarrassment. He realised with a sense of shock that he had never really regarded the landlady he saw during the day as the same woman he made love to at night.

"Where were you, Holland? I was worried to death."

He told her that he had been hiding from the police, a fact she accepted with equanimity. She let go of him and began to search for a note that had arrived for him in his absence. There was no letter from his father's people. He had no time to wonder why his allowance hadn't been sent. The note was from the Commandant and unsigned. Between the lines he could sense the heat of McDaid's anger.

"I have to go," he told Mrs Mullen. "I'll be back later for my things."

She kissed him on the mouth, and he gently broke away.

Holland wasn't sure what to do about McDaid, but the problem solved itself almost immediately. As soon as he entered the street, he heard footsteps directly behind him and a finger was jammed into the back of his neck. "Bang, bang, you're dead," said a familiar voice.

"Well, that's that, isn't it?"

"Oh no," said Caffrey waving his index finger in front of Holland's face, "it wasn't loaded."

"How did you find me?"

"You were seen at the station. The boys thought you were part of Al Smith's presidential entourage. Come on, let's go and see the boss." Caffrey put on a face and said in a wheedling voice: "He's been worried sick about you."

"What about Farkas? Has he turned up?"

"Gone without a trace, like the misht over the bog."

They walked to a building in Harcourt Street that the Movement used for training and administration. McDaid was sitting at a large mahogany desk in one of the back

125

rooms, talking to a couple of dark-haired young men, neither of whom Holland knew. Their accents were from Cork or Kerry. Everyone was puffing nervously on cigarettes: thick clouds of smoke circulated beneath the high ceiling. At first McDaid ignored him. Holland stood awkwardly beside Caffrey, his hands twitching nervously, like a schoolboy awaiting punishment, while the Commandant continued to discuss the state of training camps in the south, west. Holland barely listened. All at once McDaid was finished. He swivelled around in his chair, eyes blazing and pointed his finger at Holland.

"You! Where have *you* been, mister?"

Holland explained the details of his arrest, his decision to go underground for a couple of weeks. His voice shook as he told McDaid that he was worried that they would pin Farkas' disappearance or death on him.

McDaid was not appeased.

"Court martial. This sort of thing calls for a court martial."

Holland wasn't sure if he was bluffing but somehow in the darkness of his despair he thought of a new, more convincing explanation. He forced himself to look McDaid directly in the eyes.

"If we could speak in private," he said, "I could tell you the truth, Commandant."

"This better be good," said McDaid, glancing over towards Caffrey. He ordered the Southerners to leave but indicated that Caffrey could stay.

When they had gone, Holland said: "It's to do with Mrs Mullen. Velma."

McDaid got up and started arranging papers on his desk. Caffrey shuffled his feet as if he had just experienced a surge of energy.

"Mrs Mullen, yes," repeated McDaid.

"Well, she says she's pregnant, and the child's mine."

Caffrey hastily turned halfway around and stared out the window.

Holland continued: "I knew her husband would be coming out of jail and I thought I'd be facing a court martial because of it."

McDaid sat down heavily: "Oh, you're finished now, boy, you know that don't you? I warned you about her."

"I'm sorry."

"As well you might. If word got out.... Bedding the wife of a comrade in jail. It's very bad for morale, very bad."

"I'm prepared to pay the penalty."

"Firing squad at dawn, you mean? Then the poor child would have no father at all. I suppose it all happened casually: she just came in with the hot-water bottle and things developed from there?"

"Something like that," Holland said, his head down.

McDaid winked at Caffrey, who began to snigger uncontrollably.

"Well, believe it or not, I've heard the plot of this movie before but for some strange reason I've yet to see hide nor hair of any of Mrs Mullen's offspring. It's a well-known fact that she has a softness for young would-be heroes like yourself. I'd put it out of your mind if I were you."

McDaid grinned up at Holland, his pale eyes mischievous. He came around the desk and laid a fatherly hand on his arm. "Sit yourself down and tell me all about where you've been. Don't mind the voice; my throat's been at me for the last week or so."

The voice was friendly enough but the pupils in McDaid's eyes were needle-sharp. Holland sat down and McDaid balanced himself on the side of the desk, looking down at him, smoking a cigarette.

Holland gave a brief account of his arrest and his escape to the Midlands. He kept his sentences short, expecting to be interrupted at any moment. McDaid started to wheeze, and raised his hand at the same time. "While you've been dandering about the countryside—the girl, the Jewish girl—where's she?"

Somehow McDaid's bout of coughing made it easier to lie to him. "She left. I have no idea where she is."

There was a moment after he had said this when he knew that there still was a chance to come clean and tell them the truth. He could have said: 'I'm only joking, lads. I have her safe and sound. Just come down to Finea and pick her up.'

While he was considering this, McDaid greedily drank water from a glass on the desk and his coughing fit subsided.

"The story's like this." McDaid fingers tapped the tabletop once for each word, making Holland's eyes blink. "We think—the way it looks—that little Yiddish bitch who was working for Farkas told her friends across the water where he was and they came over and—we don't know—either plugged him or scared him off. All we know is he's gone and she's gone. And we can't touch the money we're owed. The money's still there—we think—but we can't touch it."

"What money would this be?"

McDaid turned his head sharply to one side to look at Caffrey, then returned his gaze to Holland. His eyes were acid. "Come on, Holland, you don't have to play that stupid fucking clown act with me. Caffrey must have told you at least some of it. I'm not completely thick. Eh Caffrey?"

For once Caffrey looked as if he were in earnest: "I told him nothing, Boss. I really didn't."

"To hell with this malarky. Holland, I'm going to ask you this one question. Think carefully and then answer me. All right?"

Holland nodded.

"When exactly did you last see the Jewish girl?"

Holland spoke slowly and deliberately as McDaid preferred. "She rang me up—this was before I knew that Farkas was gone—and she asked me to drive her down to the mail boat, for the night sailing. I drove back and parked the car in the garage. I went up to the office but it was locked. I went back to the digs and I was heading out to meet you when the cops picked me up and brought me to the Bridewell."

McDaid exploded. "I knew it, I knew it! She set up Farkas and then got over to England as fast as she could."

He could hardly contain himself. He marched up and down slapping his hands against his wrists.

"If she's in England, we can still get hold of her. We have her address over there. There are plenty of good men in London."

He clapped Holland on the shoulder, avuncular again.

"Don't you disappear on us again. We missed you."

"I can go now?"

"I suppose so. I have things to do." He looked at Caffrey: "Send the other two back in."

Caffrey took Holland by the arm and led him out of the room.

"The two of us should have a chat."

It was important to pretend that everything was back to normal. Holland remembered a pub they used to visit.

"What about Mulligan's?"

"Good idea, we'll take one of the snugs. I have a few things to do here first. I'll be with you in about half an hour."

Holland took a chance, extracted a cigarette from his coat pocket and lit it. His hands were quite steady.

He grinned over at Caffrey but couldn't think of a single thing to say to him.

In the relaxed ease of the snug, Caffrey stretched out his arms and glanced sideways at Holland.

Holland said: "I'll order a couple of pints." He lifted the hatch and poked out a finger.

The barman knew him. "What'll it be, Mr H?"

He ordered the drink and looked over at Caffrey.

"It was *this* close." Caffrey tried to click his fingers but failed miserably. He smiled. Holland smiled back. "They were going to put everyone on the alert. You could have been shot. The Free Staters wouldn't have bothered defending you, even if you ran into a barracks with the posse after you."

Holland felt a wave of nausea sweep over him.

"As I said, I had to get out of Dublin quick. I was sure the Special Branch weren't going to let me go like that. If they'd found Farkas' body, they'd have pinned the murder on me."

Caffrey sprawled out cat-like on the bench. Their drinks arrived and Holland placed a pint carefully in front of his friend.

Caffrey shook his head: "Well, maybe you know something I don't. But to be honest, I don't think Farkas has joined his ancestors yet. That fella's too bloody smart to get himself shot. And I'm not sure he's all that scared of this Jewish crowd either. They'd stand out like sore thumbs here anyway, unless they had someone who could pass for a Paddy and I don't think they have. Maybe Ben Briscoe."

"What happened to Farkas then?"

"He only went and scarpered, didn't he? With as much loot as he could carry. That's my guess. But the problem is: McDaid has a thing about that girl."

Holland was about to say something but Caffrey lifted up his hand to stop him.

"Look, Holly, before this goes any further, I don't want you to lie to me; about her, or about anything else. I don't want any lies between us. That's why I'm not asking any questions."

Holland's head was pounding. "That's all right with me."

"As you probably guessed, I haven't mentioned anything to McDaid about you and her. He's as innocent as the day is long. His idea of a woman is something that lies underneath his cock for a few minutes and reminds him of a map of Ireland."

Holland laughed nervously.

Caffrey continued: "And to be perfectly honest, if you don't tell me any lies, I won't have to tell him any either. Ignorance and sweet fucking bliss all round."

"I'll drink to that."

Caffrey sipped his pint.

"Did you hear that poor McCarthy got shot dead by the Special Branch?"

"I read it about it in the *Press*."

"Did you hear the really big news? It wouldn't be in the *Press*."

Holland shook his head.

Caffrey moved around to his side of the table and whispered in his ear: "Barry's resigned. At a meeting of the Army Council in Banba Hall. Sick to death of living in Dublin apparently. Fitzpatrick's the new Chief of Staff but sure all he can do is organise dances, and he's not even good at that. McDaid thinks he might have a chance himself but he needs that money. There's damn all coming through from Clan na Gael in the States these days. The Jewish girl – did she have any papers with her when you dropped her off, anything that looked like a list?"

"I thought you weren't going to ask any questions."

"Nobody's going to leave you alone on this, Holly. McDaid's turning over every word you said right now. He'll come back and ask you the same question."

"I've nothing to hide. I didn't see any lists. All she had was some luggage, a few bags. She'd hardly be waving a list in my face if it was important, would she?" Holland felt the lies coming more fluently now, and he disliked himself for it. "What was on this list?"

"Names, addresses and numbers. Everyone named and numbered. A whole flock of rich Jews in Germany were getting Farkas to liquidate their assets for them because they couldn't do it themselves. They had accounts all over the place, bonds, shares, who knows? They were trying to get out of the country but the Nazis were stealing everything, left, right and centre."

"The Special Branch are still hunting around too."

"Yeah, but they don't have a clue what's happened. It's just a disappearance to them. A company director: they're worried it'll tarnish Ireland's image abroad. But they've been looking for your girlfriend. They'll be looking in England as well—there's a lot of people who want to find out what happened to that money."

"Why are you're telling me all this now?"

"Why do you think? The game's over. McDaid'll rant and rave for a while but the money's well out of our reach and Farkas with it. Isn't it?"

"It looks like it." Afternoon light streamed in through the window at Holland's back and lit up Caffrey's face. His blue gaze shone on Holland's face as innocently as a schoolboy's. How could he not trust him?

"Remember you once asked me why I was in the Movement?" Caffrey said. "I've thought about it a lot since you disappeared on us. I think it's because it used to be so good. We were always pissing ourselves laughing then, weren't we? Remember we were down south training? Or the time in Tuam? All the competitions? Who could assemble a Lee Enfield fastest in the dark? All that shite."

"They were good times."

"Yeah, it was simple back then. We had the fascists to beat. There was fighting in the streets. Things were happening. You got a fist in the face and you thought your nose was broken, then you kicked the living shit out of the Blueshirt you'd knocked down on the ground. Life was sweet. Everything made sense."

The two men looked at each other in silence over the milky froth of their pints.

Caffrey leaned back. "Do you really think heaven is a place where people dance round on clouds? Or do you think it's like here but a little bit better?"

"Maybe there's a united Ireland in it."

"To be honest, the fun is having a cause to fight for. Doesn't really matter what the cause is, just as long as it's there."

"Caff, I get the feeling you're keeping something back."

Caffrey touched his lips with his forefinger and giggled. "McDaid told me to keep an eye on you. I wasn't supposed to tell you that, but there you are."

"What's he afraid of?"

"He's not afraid of anything; he's just obsessed with that Jewish girl and her list."

Holland took another sip of his pint. "What if I swore to you that she doesn't have the list, that she knows no more about the investments than the two of us?"

There was a long pause. Holland became aware of the voices of the other customers, the low insistent complaint of working-class Dublin speech.

Caffrey gave him a knowing look. "Yeah, that's a mighty big 'what if'. I'd trust you. I'd always trust you. But McDaid's another matter."

"You'd let me walk away? Leave the city?"

Caffrey lifted up his arms. "You're as free as a bird."

"You're serious?"

Caffrey grabbed him by the shoulders. "We're brothers, the two of us. Better than most brothers. Come on, finish your pint and we'll find an aytin' house."

They spent the rest of the evening wandering between various establishments until, half-drunk, singing the spoof Republican song, 'Holy Jesus, save us from Mother Ireland', they clambered on board the No. 23 tram that took them from the quays to Fairview where Caffrey had his digs.

Holland slept fitfully and woke early. A beam of sunlight shot through the gap between the curtains directly into his eyes. He tenderly moved Caffrey's arm, which was resting on his chest and got out of the bed. He had decided to return to Kinale but there was something he had to do, however risky, before that. Despite his grogginess, he found the road they had taken that night and managed to locate the tram terminus at Ballybough Bridge. He was back in town before Caffrey noticed he was gone.

In Stoneybatter the streets were already alive with animals and jobbers. Today it was sheep. He recalled a drover telling him that with sheep you'd think you were walking into a river—never a shadow on the ground. Today, he wanted to leave no shadow: he wanted to get in and out before anyone saw him. After the last of the tenants had left for work, he gently eased the front door open. Velma was in the kitchen cleaning up the breakfast things, singing a ditty to herself. Holland had no desire to involve her: it was best she knew nothing.

He crept up the stairs, using the banisters to take the weight off his feet. At the door of his own room he listened for a few seconds before inserting the key. The lock clicked like a pistol being taken off safety. He pushed open the door. A woman's blouse and skirt lay across the unmade bed. There was a large suitcase beside the wardrobe and some bottles of cheap scent on the bedside table.

His own things were probably in Velma's front room, not that that bothered him one way or another. He closed the door gently behind him and walked over to the corner. His fingers explored the underside of the skirting board until he found a slight depression in the wooden floor. He took a penny from his pocket and pressed hard against it; a square of skirting board came away in his hand to reveal a small hiding place inside the wall. Normally he kept the Parabellum there but all that was in it now were a few rounds of ammunition and the satchel full of papers Farkas had entrusted to him. He put the ammunition in his pockets, stuffed the satchel under his jacket and left the room and the lodging house.

On a whim, and in spite of the danger, he took the tram out to Sabine's old home, where he hoped to find some clue to Farkas' disappearance. He nourished a naïve hope that Farkas would suddenly reappear and his world would miraculously return to normal: that he could somehow have Sabine and remain in the Movement. There was no sign of life in the flat. He broke in without difficulty, but there was nothing that offered him any hope—no post, no messages, no sign of any change since Sabine had left the place.

16

The return to Kinale was not easy for Holland. He knew he was finally turning his back on the Movement.

First he had to take the train to Navan, then collect the car, which he had parked near the middle of the town where it wouldn't attract attention. Walking quickly, eyes straight ahead, he was aware of everything around him. The train journey was an action that had seemed easy to reverse. Getting into the car and driving it north and west was a much more serious step. He could feel the past breaking free and floating away from him. There was no escaping the fact that he was deliberately countermanding his orders from McDaid. He could justify his appropriation of Farkas' car the first time but a second theft would be impossible to explain. Each small town he passed through felt like a milestone on his path away from his old life. And for what reason was he doing this? He could hardly put words on it himself.

Holland continued to drive and think, smoking cigarette after cigarette, negotiating roads that grew hillier and narrower and more winding as he approached his destination. The placid midland skies, with their stately clouds chugging eastwards like barges to the cities of the coast, filled him with melancholy.

He was full of doubts, his mind lost in a forest of questions marks. When he was a child, one of his favourite stories was the tale of Hansel and Gretel. Perhaps he could follow all the cigarette butts he had cast out of the window and reverse each step of his flight from Dublin, retrace his steps to where McDaid was sitting at his desk, and tell him the truth? But however much he tried, he couldn't erase the memory of McDaid's hatred of Sabine.

It was late afternoon by the time he reached his hideaway beside Lough Sheelin's south-western shore. He reversed the Wolseley into its old tracks and covered it up as before. Hunger gnawed at him—he had not eaten all day—but cigarettes helped to ease the pangs. He took a last look at Lough Sheelin, the tiny beach of grey sand where he half expected to see miniature people cavorting, the banks of reed beds curving away from the shore, their blondness sharply contrasted with the choppy blue waters. Then he set off on foot towards Finea.

Holland collected the oars from where he had hidden them and got into FX's boat. He was so tired by now, he could do little more than steer as the current took hold and ferried him towards the lake. Somehow he managed to find the strength to row, to plunge the oars into the deep muscular tide of the lake. This was the last step in the journey.

Sabine and FX were busily picking strawberries from the garden when Holland arrived. Sabine could tell that he was exhausted.

He collapsed on the grass in front of her. "I suppose you missed me?" he asked.

Instead of a sarcastic remark, Sabine's head shyly bobbed up and down and her hair rolled down over her face. Holland felt his heart lighten. FX clapped him on the shoulder and went off to the house to put on a kettle for tea.

"I'm glad you're back," said Sabine quietly.

"I brought you a few books. They weigh a ton."

"Not from my flat? If they were watching—"

"I went in the back, over the roof of the outhouse. I couldn't see anyone near the place. If they were watching, they didn't see me."

Holland extracted a large illustrated book from the bag.

"My little *Prinzesschen in dem Wald*," Sabine cried. "How sweet! How did you know I'd want that?"

"It was your childish nature, and I liked the pictures. There wasn't time to go through all the philosophical stuff."

Sabine clasped the book to her bosom.

"It was my favourite book when I was a child. I wanted to have blonde hair like the princess and all the forest children."

Suddenly there was a catch in Sabine's voice. She looked at him with glistening eyes. "The other books I have are just for reading. This one is for remembering." She placed the book carefully back inside the satchel. "Did you talk to Mrs Fitzgibbons?"

"No. I decided not to risk it."

Sabine gently reached over and touched his arm. "Thank you for thinking of me."

To get back to the house, they had to walk along the narrow furrows between the rows of vegetables. Holland stumbled and Sabine reached out her hand to catch him. Their hands stayed joined—awkwardly, self-consciously—for an instant longer than necessary.

At dinner that evening, Holland and Sabine barely opened their mouths, either to speak or to eat. Their eyes met as they passed potatoes to each other or casually scanned the room. FX noticed the change in atmosphere.

The food, which Sabine had spent so much time over, tasted of ashes in his mouth. The older man felt intensely the emptiness of his own life, sensed acutely that the fires that once had filled him were dying away into the dark.

17

Holland and FX were arguing about de Valera. It was late in the evening but the sun still shone with unusual brilliance through the grey windows of the kitchen.

FX was leaning across the table. His colour was high and his thick grey eyebrows rose up like hairy wings over the agitated face.

"De Valera might be an undertaker but that's what we need at the moment. You don't see it yet? But there has to be someone to bury the old hate. If we don't, we'll be forced to make all the same mistakes again."

Holland leaned back in his chair, his legs sprawled in front of him.

"What about the occupied Six Counties? You'd turn your back on them?"

"Sure, they've always been occupied. We were always occupied: when were we not? What does 'occupied' mean anyway? A human being can only occupy one portion of space at a time. We should just hold on to what we've got while we've got it. That's what life is: holding your ground."

"When you're dead, you can hold your ground. When you're alive, you have to move. You've bought the pro-British argument, FX. All we'll get is the status quo."

"That's where you're wrong. Our power is limited. But the fact is that you could do what you want in this

140

country, get some industry going in it, and matter a damn if there are a few British parasites sitting at the top. Once you've built the place up, then you can start moving things."

Holland did not feel like arguing any more. Talk was a waste of time. Either the people of the South awakened and took back the Northern counties or they didn't. He rose from the table and examined the amount of groceries left in the cupboards.

"And another thing," continued FX, as though the argument were still in full swing. "We're running out of food. All we have left is a few spuds and some cabbage."

It was becoming impossible to shop for someone like Sabine without attracting attention in a place as small as Abbeylara, and there was a limit to how far they could travel by bicycle. Granard was several miles away and Longford even farther.

"There's only one thing for it," Holland said.

Late that night, he cycled out to Lough Sheelin, disrobed the Wolseley of its camouflage of branches and leaves and drove it back to the farm. The bike rattled like a demon from the boot. He had not brought enough string to tie it down properly, so he slowed down to a crawl each time he passed a house on the road. On the last part of the journey, he stopped the engine and pushed the Wolseley down the lane leading to FX's house. Sweat was pouring down his face by the time he parked the car beside one of the outhouses. He stood looking at it for a while, with only the stars as witnesses, and felt for the first time that he had finally broken free of the Movement.

The following morning FX marched around the car in his badly frayed wellingtons.

"My God, it's nearly new, and it's big. The locals will want you to take them for spins in it."

"That's exactly why I didn't want to drive it over here."

"We can keep it in the old byre there at the back. If we clear out the rubbish there'll be room. No one need know it's here."

"They'll find out eventually," Holland said. For the first time, he realised that their stay would have to be short.

He took FX to Granard to buy groceries the following day. They started early in the morning to avoid being seen locally. In his inside pocket, Holland carried a list that Sabine had written out. He didn't understand half the things that were on it but she had agreed to cook for them if they brought home the ingredients she needed. They motored up and down the countryside for a couple of hours before entering Granard. It was a chore for Holland but FX acted like a schoolboy. In Granard the shopkeepers shook their heads in puzzlement when they read out many of the items on Sabine's list.

The two men gamely got into the car and drove all the way to Longford, a much bigger town. Sabine craved fruit, vegetables, herbs and tinned goods that country people in Ireland had no knowledge of. They found most of them in Longford, a town that received regular deliveries by rail from Dublin. But there were some things Holland could not bear to buy Sabine. These were the cotton towels she needed to protect her clothes when she was having her period. He stood outside the chemist's and he stood outside the ladies' hosiery, but no amount of willpower could make him put his foot over the doorstep to ask for these items.

When they returned late that evening, worn out from their long trek from shop to shop and all the baffled looks and sounds of exasperation from the shop attendants, Sabine was waiting for them outside the back door, her hair loose, her slim figure silhouetted by the headlamps, like a statue of the Madonna. She eagerly examined all the things they had bought. Her hands delved into each of the bags and pulled up the contents as though they were trophies. It was only after she had gone through everything and asked if there was anything else that Holland admitted to her that he had not bought the cotton cloths.

"I could take you in next week. If you stay in the back of the car for the first few miles, no one will notice."

"You don't understand, stupid man! I need those things now."

As Sabine grew more heated, FX's eyes strayed to the ceiling and he quickly vacated the room.

Holland felt angry and ashamed. He was prepared to face death, to walk into an open field against armed men, but he lacked the courage to buy a few pieces of cloth. He bit his lip and listened, without uttering a word, to Sabine's tirade.

Afterwards, they ate in silence the meal Sabine had prepared for them. She walked out and left them before they had gathered up the plates.

Sabine felt deeply alone with her women's troubles. She tore up some old sheets she found upstairs but the material was not very absorbent. As soon as she could, she went down to the cottage by the lake and spent a long, lonely night trying to ignore the dismal creaking of the corncrakes and the slow insistent melody of the wind in the trees. Her body seemed to be fighting against her; the cramps were worse than she remembered. She felt she was the last woman on earth, trapped amongst ignorant men who could not sum up the courage to walk into a shop and speak to an assistant.

When she finally fell asleep, her dreams were full of creatures from the horror stories of the Polish *shtetl*. Witches and demons roamed the boglands. Great clay giants with unseeing eyes marched through the Irish woods. Slime-covered creatures with teeth of iron crawled out of the lake. Holland tried to hold them off, firing round after round from his Parabellum. FX incanted Latin phrases from the odes of Horace, but they continued their hideous march to the cottage. The nightmarish creatures stood at her window, their eyes burning like torches through the glass, their huge red mouths slavering.

Sabine awoke in a fright, drenched in sweat. Keeping her eyes from the windows, she looked down at the bed. Her groin was plastered with sticky, dried blood. She climbed carefully out from beneath the bedclothes and placed her feet on the floor. The previous night she had had the foresight to fill a tin basin with water. She attempted to scrub off the blood. The hard soap did not lather; the water rapidly stained. Tears of frustration burst from her eyes. It was early in the morning shortly after sunrise. The dawn chorus was at its loudest. Sabine coiled a blanket around herself and walked down to the shore of the lake, holding a bar of soap and a towel in her free hand. It was cold but bearable: she felt so unclean that she wanted to plunge straight into the water immediately and swim far into the lake.

Instead, she carefully divested herself of the blanket and walked over the flat stones until the water reached her midriff. She lathered herself and watched as the blood sank down to the sandy bottom while the suds rose into a cloud-like froth below the surface.

When Sabine had finished and was about to wade back to the shore, she felt a sudden fear. Someone, she was sure, was watching her. She recalled her dream, the burning eyes at the windows, but she was now more fearful of being watched by the local Irish than the creatures of Polish nightmares.

She peered through the early morning mist into the surrounding fields and woods until, close by, she discovered the curious stare of a large pair of brown eyes. At first, she took it to be a giant rabbit, as though the richness of the grassland had created monsters even of such harmless creatures, but it was nothing but a hare.

"*Der kleinen Löffelzwerg,*" she said to herself, laughing, and when she had waded back to the shore, and had wrapped the blanket about her, she shouted out the words as though to exorcise all the demons of the previous night. Her words returned in echoes from the other side of the lake. She remembered her nakedness and, filled with a sudden exhilaration, rushed back to the cottage, stumbling over the rounded bodies of the stones as she ran.

18

Their lives were very quiet for the next few days. Sabine helped FX in his vegetable garden. Holland carried out repairs on the cottage and went fishing on the lake. Often it rained: a steady grey downpour, which turned the backyard to mud, swamped the freshly planted shoots in the garden, and churned up the smooth surface of the lake. With some help from Holland, Sabine managed to tune the wireless to a German station and she spent hours listening to news reports and music programmes.

One morning Holland awoke early, his mouth dry. He could hear his uncle's disjointed proprietary snores coming from the next room and decided he might as well get up. He lit the fire in the kitchen with some loose pages from a newspaper and boiled up the kettle. Outside, the birds were ecstatically calling to each other from the deep bushes that encircled the house. The sounds of creaking from the landing told him that his uncle too was awake. After building up the fire, he put a pot of water on the hob and started hunting around for a bag of oatmeal. He intended to impress FX with a fresh bowl of porridge. Holland found the bag in a cupboard and for some reason, on the way over to the stove, was captivated by the tiny patch of shimmering grey light in the distance.

"Quite a sight, Kinale; it used to be anyway," said FX from a spot immediately behind him. "In the winter if it was stormy, the waves would be topped with white, like horses. Always reminded me of the ocean."

"That's hard to imagine," said Holland.

"Ah, you don't remember how it used to be. How could you? All those bushes and bits of trees have blocked off the view. The years…"

"My mother would have spent time looking at the lake, I suppose?"

"She would have, yes. Your mother liked looking at nature, God bless her soul."

They had just started eating their breakfast when they heard a car coming down the lane at speed and then screeching to a halt at the back door. Holland reacted immediately: he put down his bowl and spoon and retired to the sitting room where he extracted the Parabellum from its hiding place beneath the sofa and shoved a magazine into the butt.

There he stood waiting, unsure whether to try to escape out through the window or stand his ground. He hoped that Sabine had not decided to come up to the house. If he attempted to warn her now, he would probably just draw them to where she was staying. He cursed himself for not being more alert, for not having a plan of escape.

The seconds passed. There was the sound of voices: FX's even speech and the deeper, more agitated tone of a stranger. Holland relaxed and pushed the gun under a copy of *The Irish Press* on the settee table. When he heard the door slam shut, he ventured back into the kitchen.

FX was sitting at the table drinking his tea and staring absent-mindedly out of the window. After they heard the car drive away, he turned to Holland and said: "That was

Father Carney, the parish priest. What on earth was your girlfriend doing gallivanting around buck-naked? Does she think this place is a nudist camp?"

Holland ran his knuckles along the top of the table, and kept his eyes averted.

"Lucky for you—and for me—that I know all about young Duffy, the one who saw her. He's a bit simple but you can usually rely on what he says. I told the priest he was talking about mermaids the other week. If I've contributed to having him sent away, I'll have a hard time forgiving myself. But your friend should have thought of that too."

"She knows nothing about life here."

"Maybe you should have given her a few lessons. Bathing in the nude beside the house, in full view! If she'd gone further down the shore, no one would have seen her, but *here*! Go down and speak to her. We can't have another visit from the clergy. If it happens just once more, if she's as much as seen by somebody other than Duffy, we'll be in for it."

Holland turned his head and made for the door. He was not used to seeing FX in a temper.

"Hold on, hold on, don't take what I say so seriously, Orwen. I'm always on edge with that priest, snooping into everything."

"You have the right to say what you want. It's your place; you have to live here when we're gone."

"It's not that. It's this country. Do you recall that fella that lived up the road, Iggy Lynch? He used to swing you till you were dizzy when you were small?"

"Yeah, Iggy. He never got tired. What about him?"

"I found him. About a month ago, it would be. We had to break down the door. He was half-eaten by the rats, his face gone. That's the way we end here. And all the priest has to do with his time is chase round the country closing down dance halls and flushing couples out of the hedges. And then he has the cheek to advise the young to leave for England."

"I'll go down and have a word with Sabine. I can take her some breakfast."

FX looked kindly upon him. "You can say, if she wants to do—you know—that sort of thing, she should go further down the shore. No one will see her on that stretch of the lake."

Holland filled up a bowl with porridge and milk and covered it with another to keep it warm. He left the house and began to make his way to the cottage, but before he had gone more than a hundred yards, FX shouted for him to return. He trudged back wondering if FX expected him to balance a cup of tea on top of the bowl.

In the kitchen FX stood by the table gingerly holding the Parabellum by the muzzle.

"I found this in the sitting room. I don't suppose I have to ask if it's yours?"

"It's mine. It's a Parabellum."

"Ah yes," said FX frowning, "*si vis pacem para bellum.* Have you ever heard that? No? It means, *if you desire peace, prepare for war.*"

"It's a weapon, FX. I need it to protect Sabine."

"Don't use a woman to make your excuses. I just wonder how many lives have been taken by this thing. Did no one ever tell you fellas that the war is over?"

Holland refused to be drawn in. He put down the porridge bowl and stuck his hands awkwardly into his pockets.

"You're still one of the boys, aren't you? It was my hospitality," FX said, his voice quivering, "my hospitality you have abused, turning me into a hypocrite in front of my neighbours. I have only ever preached peace, and here I am harbouring a gunman. You have made a liar out of me." He placed the gun on the tabletop and sank down into a chair as though the wind had gone out of him. "Your mother, God rest her soul… she wanted you to make something of yourself. She would have been very sorely disappointed...." His voice trailed off.

Holland walked over and picked up the gun.

"We'll be gone by tomorrow," he said.

FX looked up at him, his eyes mild again, and filled with sadness. He had never had any faculty for losing his temper. He had never had any children of his own.

"Have you nothing else to say, Orwen?"

"Our war isn't over yet, FX. I still need this."

19

Under a perfect azure sky they made their preparations. Sabine packed her belongings in the boot. Then she walked around the cottage one last time, making sure that everything was in place and the windows securely shut. Holland checked the engine of the Wolseley while FX baked soda bread and farls for the journey. In front of the car FX had placed a small pile of vegetables: carrots, potatoes and a head of cabbage.

When Holland went into the kitchen, he slapped his uncle on the back. "We won't be needing vegetables where we're going. Sabine is heading for the boat. She'll look a bit of an eejit walking around with a cabbage and a bag of carrots."

FX screwed up his face. "You never know what you'll need out there. Anyway, it'd make her look more rural."

Holland couldn't tell whether FX was relieved to see them go or just putting a brave face on their departure. He would return to his lonely furrow again, filling the days with his books, the cultivation of his vegetables and an occasional trip on the lake to fish. How anyone could accept such a life was a mystery to Holland: even in the Movement, where Volunteers had to live with the constant danger of death or imprisonment, there was never the possibility of loneliness.

Sabine stared across the lake for what she thought was the last time, her eyes hypnotised by the tiny shards of sunlight dancing across its surface. A coot scolded from the impenetrably thick reed beds on the far side, and a grebe sat motionless on the water about fifty yards from where she was standing. Suddenly the grebe upended and dived. The movement was quicker than thought; and afterwards there was barely a ripple on the surface of the water. Sabine began to count the seconds: *ein tausend, zwei tausend, drei tausend* … the German words sounding heavy and earth-like in such a setting. She continued until she grew tired of counting and her voice faded away. The grebe had disappeared into a magical realm of its own.

She heard Holland's voice calling her and took the path to the house. All this will continue, she thought, after I have gone. No trace of me will be left here.

Sabine put her luggage into the boot and sat in the passenger seat. Holland looked embarrassed. "I'll have to get you to lie down in the back until we can put a few miles between us and the house. As a precaution."

She nodded and awkwardly got out. FX came shyly over to offer his hand. His blue eyes looked intensely child-like in the strong sunlight, and Sabine felt a motherly sympathy for him. This sort of loneliness was almost tangible and as soon as they went, it would reclaim him. She opened her arms and hugged him.

"There's some soda bread and a bottle of tea on the backseat," FX said in a croaky voice, "in case you get thirsty."

Holland made his farewell casually: he shook FX's hand with a quick deft motion. Then he sat in the driver's seat, relieved to be finally on the move again, and gunned the car into life. The Wolseley lurched and bucked over the sun-hardened dips and crests of the lane while FX watched, hands securely fastened to the insides of his pockets. Sabine waved her hand

mechanically, before disappearing into the dark ano-
nymity of the backseat.

Holland drove without feeling the need to say anything. With nothing to look at but the bare leather of
the backseat, Sabine felt like screaming. For a time she
amused herself by watching the tiny bubbles rising in
the milky tea and dissipating into air inside the stormy
neck of the bottle. Her pride would not allow her be the
first to speak but, after some time had elapsed, she suc-
cumbed and asked Holland if it was safe to sit up.

"Are you getting bored down there?"

Sabine ground her teeth and waited. Holland opened
the window and checked the mirrors.

"The problem is that there are eyes everywhere. A
car like this will always attract attention."

"Well, talk to me then."

"There's not much to tell you. I can see a lot of people out helping with the hay. They're building a hay reek
in the corner of a field."

"A hay reek?"

"It's a local way of drying hay."

"How long will it take us until we reach the next
town?"

"Depends on the traffic. There are a lot of farmers
moving hay."

Sabine forced herself to relax and must have dozed
off because when Holland spoke again, they were coming into Oldcastle.

In contrast to the last time they were there, the
town was full of carts and farmers. Holland had deliberately chosen to fill the tank up in Oldcastle because
the market would make them less obvious, but he hadn't
expected the town to be this crowded. The traffic was so
dense that they ended up parking on one of the streets

that fed into the square, next to a line of carts resting on their shafts.

"You can sit up now."

Sabine pulled herself into a sitting position. "Where's the petrol station?"

"In the square. I don't see how we can get past all this. We'll have to wait a few minutes."

He was relieved to see that theirs was not the only car in town. Parked on the corner was a Morris.

With a start, Holland noticed that there was a man sitting in the front seat.

"Stay close to the car. I'm going to have a look at our friend on the other side of the road."

"Is he a policeman?"

"I don't think so. He'd be showing more interest in us if he were."

As Sabine watched, Holland pushed his way through the crowd towards the car. The driver did not seem to be interested in anything going on in the street. He simply stared straight ahead as if he were a dummy.

Holland walked as far as the next street and then returned. "Worn clothes, stained hands. He's either a mechanic or a labourer. Harmless," he told Sabine.

"How does that tell you he's harmless?"

"The dangerous ones in this country are the ones with the lily-white hands—the priests and the police."

"What do we do now?"

"Wait."

They sat in the car at the edge of the market as though spellbound. It was a street full of men, some young and fresh-faced, the majority gnarled by years of rain and sun, all dressed almost identically in dark suits and cloth caps, their black bikes left unlocked, leaning in orderly clerical lines against every available wall. The older countrymen fascinated Sabine: their skin, especially at the nape, like parchment etched with ancient script. The Irish in this place appeared to be the last remnants of some ancient race, the original European *Urvolk*, before it fractured into myriad tribes, perhaps even a lost tribe of Israel. Compared to them, the Germans seemed factory new, a shallow and aggressive variant.

She examined the carts parked on either side of the street.

"Do they only sell pigs here?"

"This is pig market day: tomorrow they'll sell giraffes and then on Friday, elephants."

"You think you're so funny." Holland cast a look in her direction. There was a faint smile.

"I'm going to have to break up a five pound note at the bank to buy petrol. It's all I've got and it'll draw attention to us if they can change it at all."

Sabine was suddenly stern. "No, you must stop paying for me. I have enough money in my purse. Believe me, please."

"Keep it. You'll need your money when you get to England."

"I insist. It's not for discussion," Sabine said, her eyes excited, as she handed him a ten-shilling note.

Holland closed his eyes; he was never sure how to deal with Sabine's volatile temper but he had no intention of allowing her to pay.

"Look, Sabine, I *have* to pay. Otherwise I'll never get rid of you. It's as simple as that. You'll just end up back here again." He looked at her and smiled broadly, a cue to indicate that his remark was meant to be funny. But Sabine did not get the hint. Holland might as well have slapped her in the face. She felt her carefully composed exterior fall away. Her feelings were suddenly nakedly exposed in front of this brutal mocking stranger in this brutal pig-breeding, pig-eating country. The blood drained from her face and she experienced an overwhelming urge to run from the car and bury herself in the earth. She withdrew the proffered note and automatically put it in her purse.

"Yes, I understand," she muttered.

Holland nodded, happy that he had got through to her.

"Is there a railway station in this town?" Sabine asked.

"Yes, out toward the Ballyjamesduff road. Don't worry though; we'll be able to get petrol."

He got out of the car and pulled on his heavy great-coat, even though the day was warm. His suit was too Dublin; the dark colour of the coat would help him blend in. He wandered past row after row of carts and pig-pens and the odd lorry. Occasionally someone looked up and scanned his face. Holland could feel eyes follow him as he pushed through the crowd towards the Northern Bank. He was aware that he didn't quite fit in.

The bank was thronged with dark-suited men, the smell of unwashed bodies reminding him of the back rows of the church. He stood in a straggling queue, wondering how pushy he could afford to be without attracting attention.

"Grand day, grand day altogether," exclaimed the man in front of him when he accidentally shoved against his arm.

He worried about Sabine trapped in the car, suddenly alone in this sea of men. Perspiration gathered on his nape. To occupy himself, he imagined disassembling the gun. And then, as if his mind had made his thoughts concrete, this image of a gun became real.

A slight young man with a lick of dark hair over his forehead was waving a Browning automatic and roaring at everyone to stand over by the wall. Two other armed men ran in from the square and with kicks and oaths made the customers move aside. Pressed against the other men, he felt the intolerable heat of his coat, so much so that at first he paid scant attention to the bank robbers. He forced himself to look.

None of the men wore masks. Their bloodless faces were intense and their eyes inhabited by a peculiar innocence, the savage innocence of youthful idealism. They were all Republicans, he was certain of it, collecting funds for the Movement. With a shock he realised that he knew one of them by name. The third in, the skinniest man, Fallon, he had trained in small arms use. He could even remember trying to teach him how to assemble a Webley, the boy's nervous energy spoiling every effort he made to fit the intricate mechanism together.

It was so peculiar seeing them there, like running into distant members of one's family, that he felt a desire to make himself known to them, to shout a name. But this proved unnecessary. He too had been recognised. Fallon made a signal to him and pulled him away into a corner, the Browning loosely directed at his crotch. Holland hoped that he had had the sense to keep it on safety.

Fallon whispered: "Pretend you don't know me; show me anything you've got in your pockets." Holland turned out his pockets and his comrade pretended to look at what he produced: a comb, some bills and his driving licence. "What are you doing here? Everyone is looking for you? Some say you were arrested or even shot. I also heard you were signed up by the Staters."

"I've been lying low. I can't trust anyone."

"You know you'll have to fucking well trust me, and I'll have to tell HQ. It'd be better for you if you reported in first. Here's your stuff; go back to the others."

Holland hitched his arms into the air and moved crabwise back to the heaving tide of suited men.

The three raiders backed out as smoothly as they had entered, one of them carrying a bag stuffed with money. He heard a single shot from the square. They were either scaring away the local constabulary or just trying to clear the crowd. He knew their next step would be to get as far from Oldcastle as possible within the next hour and then lie low in a safe house for a few days until the guards and the army got tired of the chase. The problem for Holland was that he and Sabine could easily get caught in the slow relentless drag-net that would inevitably follow. He knew that de Valera's new men in the Special Branch would do their utmost to prove that they were cracking down on their former comrades.

Holland pushed through the crowds that had gathered about the bank, evaded the guards who were already rapidly moving into the square, and walked as casually as possible back to the place where he'd parked the car. Their only hope was to drive away from the town as fast as possible. Apart from the car belonging to the bank raiders, theirs was probably the only strange vehicle in the town. The first thing he noticed was that the Morris had gone. This had been the raiders' getaway car, he thought. The young man in the driving seat had been stiff with fear.

This new information made it even harder to walk at a normal pace towards the Wolseley but he managed it somehow. When he got close enough to see through the haze of reflections obscuring the windscreen, he came to a dead stop. Sabine wasn't there. He looked wildly around. There was no sign of her on the street. He waited a couple of seconds, paralysed by indecision. Where was she? Had the Guards picked her up? He couldn't imagine it. He tried to visualise what she would do. And it occurred to him with a feeling of dread where she might be. He recalled the way she had looked at him. She had felt insulted, and he knew she had enough money to buy a ticket to Dublin. She'd teach him a lesson and leave him without encumbering him any further. Holland resisted the temptation to run. He was aware that it might already be too late. The Guards would interview anyone taking the train and Sabine could never pass for a local. She didn't even have any luggage: all her things were locked in the boot.

For a second he followed a woman with hair as dark as Sabine's but then in time noticed the pale skin. Frantically shoving his way through a thick mass of men, he turned down the street to the station. He ran into the tiny wooden building that served as a station hall, and it was there he caught sight of her, standing at the ticket booth talking animatedly to an official. He grabbed her arm but Sabine immediately pulled it away.

She glared at him, her eyes black with anger. "Leave me alone. I will go on my own."

Holland caught the eye of the official, a middle-aged man with a reddish-grey moustache. He raised his eyebrows and smiled conspiratorially.

"Just a tiff."

The official winked and rested his elbows against the counter as though preparing himself for a long wait.

Holland put his mouth up against Sabine's ear as she violently attempted to push herself away from him again. "They're here, the police. After us."

His words did not have the desired effect. Sabine continued to shove him away. What was worse, she had begun to speak in German.

Holland forced his mouth up against her ear again; it was almost a kiss this time. "I'm sorry about what I said.

I didn't mean it. Will you come with me?" Suddenly her arm went limp; she stopped struggling and came meekly after him. He grasped her arm and thrust it into his. She did not protest.

They made their way through the crowd. In the square, policemen were interviewing members of the public on the steps of the bank. Holland told her about the raid and how important it was to get away from the town. They hurried back to the street where the car was parked. A guard was standing beside it making a note of the number plate. Holland quickly turned around and led Sabine away. For once he felt desperate. He had no idea what to do. The other customers would remember his conversation with Fallon: he could easily be picked out and taken in for questioning. There was nowhere for a man and a woman to go in a town of this size. They were strangers; they had no business being here. It would just be a matter of time before they were stopped.

"The hotel," said Sabine.

"What!"

"There, the Napper Arms. We go in there and wait until we can get back to the car."

She took Holland by the arm and swung him in the direction of the hotel, situated directly beside the bank. They nodded vaguely to the guards who were interviewing passers-by; one of the policemen even tipped his hat to them, presumably under the assumption that they were tourists. In the plush darkness of the lounge they ordered coffee and sat by the window. There were only a few other guests: wealthy farmers drinking whiskey and talking in short rapid sentences about the raid as though it had been a well-executed manoeuvre on the football field.

"They won't catch them by quizzing people in the street," one said.

"Ah sure those lads; they have half an hour of a lead on them. They managed to get out of the town in a good strong motorcar."

"Over £700 they lifted. It was the boys themselves who did it. Short of cash. It'll all end up in their coffers all right."

Holland felt nervous, trapped. Their talk seemed to implicate him too. But Sabine's presence calmed him. She took the pot of coffee from the waiter and began to pour. Her eyes closed as she raised her cup. There was something so normal and civilised about the way she was relishing the first cup of coffee she'd had since they had left Dublin that he felt all danger to be temporarily banished. She had convinced herself that they were ordinary people enjoying a break in a rural hotel.

"I'm sorry about what happened earlier. I really didn't want to take your money. That was all," Holland said.

Sabine gave him a sideways look: "You said you wanted to get rid of me. That's all right. But the look you gave me; I remember the last time that happened in Germany."

"What do you mean?"

"You have no idea, do you?"

"I try my best. I'm not always able to understand the way you think."

Sabine put down her cup and looked Holland in the eye.

"You really didn't mean any harm? You even like looking after me."

"I want to look after you. And" —his heart beat faster— "I do like you."

"I'm sorry. Perhaps I am oversensitive. I saw that look, and heard your words and remembered how it was."

"How it was in Germany?"

Sabine took a sip from her cup. "I tried to learn to exist with it. Before, when I was growing up, if you spoke German properly, were a cultivated person, then you were a German; but later, when the National Socialists came to power, that wasn't enough. It was the outer appearance that mattered: your eyes, your skin, your hair. And your name, of course. You could not save yourself by talking. It did not matter how educated you were, if you had read Goethe, Rilke to the end. They knew what you were. They didn't have to say anything, their eyes told you: 'Look—a Jew'. It was like you were made of a thousand stories, all bad or funny. Even when they welcomed you, their eyes said: 'Here is a Jew. Watch her.'"

"Why? What have the Jews done to them?"

Sabine wrinkled her nose and took another sip of her coffee. "Who knows? They hate us. It's as old as religion."

"Will you ever go back?"

"I don't think I can. I just hope my family can get out. My brother Markus, he'll escape. Do you know he had TB once? My parents sent him to Switzerland to a clinic." Sabine began to giggle like a schoolgirl. "They put him and another boy in beds outside in the snow. The idea was he would lie very still and breathe the cold air and get better. But he and this other boy, they hid their clothes in the bed with some money; and every night they climbed over the wall of the clinic and went down to the local town for a beer or to dance."

Sabine laughed so hard she nearly spilled her coffee. The men at the bar glanced cautiously over.

"He got better then, all the same?"

"Yes, of course. That is the point of the story. He'll always escape. He'll always do what they don't expect. Like me."

Holland gulped down the rest of his coffee, hardly aware of anything but its bitterness.

"I think it's time we got out of this town. We'll see if that guard is gone."

Holland paid at the counter and they both left. The market appeared to be winding down. Most of the black-suited men had left and even the pubs appeared quieter. They walked close to a cartload of pigs. The tiny human-like eyes of the cargo turned to stare at them as they passed, but the smell was not as bad as Sabine had expected. They found the car and approached it as slowly and casually as they could. A note had been stuck underneath the wind-screen wiper, asking the owner to report to the local Garda station. Holland picked it up and stuck it in his pocket. "I'll give this to Farkas next time I run into him."

He began to feel more optimistic as soon as he managed to get the engine started. They drove back the way they had come through the square, past the pigs and down the road leading to Kells and Dublin, in what they hoped was the opposite direction of the bank raiders. They passed the last row of houses, overtook another cartload of pigs and Holland began to feel that they were making a good escape.

"What about the petrol?" asked Sabine.

"We've enough to take us to the nearest town."

On the long sloping road leading to Kells, their luck changed. Holland spotted a black car already past the top of the hill and rapidly coming towards them.

"Who is it?"

Holland narrowed his eyes. "Could be an insurance salesman, a priest, a doctor, a shopkeeper, a vet or—"

"Or?"

"Or the cops, Broy's men. There's a road to the left I could take, but it's further up the hill. I'm not sure we can make it that far."

Sabine could already distinguish the dark official suit of one of its occupants. "They might just pass us to go into the village."

Holland grunted and strained at something he had hidden under his seat.

"Sabine. Can you reach it—the gun. Pull it out gently and stick it behind my back."

"You're not…."

"Just do as I say. In the small of my back. Everything will be all right."

It looked at first as if they would simply drive past. Sabine noted the large man in the front passenger seat, made even more bulky by his Garda uniform. She imagined them continuing into the village, but as Holland was changing down a gear to cope with the hill, long before he reached the turn-off on the left, the policeman suddenly stuck his hand out of the window and began to wave them to a stop. Thirty yards away the black car veered directly in front of them and came to a halt. Holland braked sharply and pulled in to the side, bumping the car onto the brow of a grass verge. The policeman got out and lumbered towards them.

He was a man in his mid-forties, heavily built and well over six feet tall. But he didn't appear to be armed. There were three stripes on his jacket. He looked formidable enough but Holland's eyes were fixed on the plain-clothes driver, who looked suspiciously like one of Broy's Special Branch men.

"You'll not shoot, Holland, please!" Sabine's voice was a whispered shriek. The dark uniform terrified her.

Holland placed his hand on her leg. "Don't worry. Have faith." For the first time that day Holland felt calm. In fact, he was looking forward to this moment. The fleshy face of the approaching policeman even reminded him comically of the faces of the pigs in the market. Come on, he thought, come on pigface, and do your stuff.

The sergeant scrutinised them as he sauntered over and Holland could see that he didn't regard them as much of a threat. All the same, they risked being brought to the station where their identities would be easy to ascertain. Holland smiled at the Garda as he loomed over the open window. He looked closely at Sabine, and despite her nervousness, Sabine smiled back.

"Licence please."

"Is it about the bank raid in town?"

The sergeant thumbed through the proffered licence but made no comment.

"Would you mind stepping out of the car?"

Holland opened the door and got out of the car, still smiling, and in one fluid movement pulled the Parabellum from behind his back and thrust it into the sergeant's abdomen. He took him completely by surprise: the little piggy eyes opened wide and there came a resounding fart from his behind. Because the sergeant was standing directly in front of him, Holland knew that the driver of the other car couldn't see the gun.

He glanced quickly over to Sabine, whose face had suddenly turned a sallow pale, and said: "Wind up the window and lock the door. Now!" and then thrust the Parabellum even deeper into the sergeant's belly. "Keep your hands at your side, Sergeant. Now tell me, is your friend back there carrying a shooter?"

The sergeant grunted something that Holland didn't catch.

"Tell me now! If you don't, I'll have to plug you right here and now. That's the way it works."

Holland's threat made little sense but he had discovered that logical arguments were unnecessary when one was pointing a gun at somebody's gut.

"He has a revolver," gasped the Sergeant.

"And there's probably a shotgun under the backseat?"

The sergeant shook his head. Holland believed him. In any case he had got most of the information he needed. He made as if to turn but instead rammed the butt of the pistol with full force into the sergeant's stomach. The man had no time to react and went down as though poleaxed. Holland shouldered him to one side and immediately began to sprint directly towards the other car. With his head down, he could see the driver fumbling in fatal slowness with some object in front of him. But Holland was too fast for him. Ten yards away he stopped abruptly, grasped the Parabellum with both hands and shot out the windscreen. When he got to the car, the detective lay sprawled and quivering on the seat, his face bleeding from the impact of shattered glass, his revolver halfway under the seat with a few bullets scattered beside it. Holland hauled the detective, who was short and slight, out by his hair and ordered him to lie face down on the road. The sergeant, meanwhile, had recovered sufficiently from the blow in the stomach to begin to zigzag in comical lurches down the hill in search of help. Holland placed his foot on the detective's shoulder and took careful aim. The bullet grazed the tarmac about a foot in front of the escaping man.

"I have six rounds left, Sergeant," he shouted. "and I'm a champion shot at thirty yards."

The sergeant halted and, clutching his belly, swung around to face Holland. Stooped over, he raised his hands as far as he could and began to walk back up the hill. When he reached the car, Holland told him to take off his belt and made him lie down beside the detective. He then extracted the belt from the detective's trench coat. The men, realising that they wouldn't be shot, cursed him fluently under their breath. Holland just laughed and bound their arms together, placing his foot unceremoniously in the small of their backs as he did so. After he had done that, he opened the hood and ripped out the distribution cap, effectively disabling their car.

Sabine watched from the Wolseley, not daring to look up or down the hill in case another vehicle was coming. Despite herself, she had felt impressed. Holland, who normally seemed so lethargic, could move with the fluidity of a big cat when he had to.

Holland returned to the car and placed the gun under his seat as though it were a simple tool of his trade.

"We'll have to get out of here fast."

Holland revved the engine and took the car into the middle of the road. The two men lying on their bellies struggled and shouted at them as they passed, their faces distorted by rage and humiliation.

The sergeant roared: "You'll get your sixteen lines," and Holland looked knowingly at Sabine and smiled. Their car gradually ascended the steep hill, its engine straining as they neared the top.

"Sixteen lines? What does it mean?"

"If you're executed, it's the maximum number of lines they can write about you in the papers."

"Would they execute you for what you did?"

"I don't think so, not these days. I'd have to have plugged one of them."

"Have you ever killed anyone?"

Holland ignored the question and looked out the window.

"Do you remember I woke you up to show you the view up here?"

Sabine recalled the dawn that morning. Life had already become much more complicated. But she could not find any words to say to Holland: her mind was too full of images from his attack on the policemen. Her stomach was still knotted with tension and she could not stop flexing and unflexing her hands. In Berlin, the people she had known would abandon the pavement to allow a man in uniform to walk past. Authority was absolute. If one crossed them, there was never any escape. And yet Holland had casually swept these servants of the state aside and while everything he had done replayed itself in her head, like a piece of film, Holland himself seemed unconcerned. He was probably a killer. A brute, she thought, an uncivilised brute.

She looked across at him. "Your hand's bleeding."

"Nothing but a flesh wound, as they say in the pictures. From the glass in the car. I must've cut myself when I hauled the little guy up by the hair."

"You really have no respect for authority, do you?"

"Authority! Those clowns!" Holland laughed. "Do you want to know something? The sergeant there probably served most of his time under the British, suppressing the people who now run this country. The other little skitter used to be in the IRA. I saw him once at a meeting in Banba Hall. So he's a turncoat. What's left to respect?"

Sabine bit her lip. "I don't understand this country."

"Well, there you are; you've just become a bit more Irish."

"What about Dublin? Could we reach it?"

Holland pointed to the foot of the hill. "Do you see that lorry there starting up the hill? He'll pass us in five minutes and reach our friends on the road in about ten, fifteen minutes. Ten minutes after that they'll be in Oldcastle where they'll alert every station in the area. I wouldn't put our chances of even getting to Kells very high, never mind Dublin. On top of that, we haven't enough petrol."

"Do you regret not shooting them?"

Holland gave Sabine a sour look. "What do you take me for? Remember I'm the cowboy in the white shirt."

Sabine smiled. "But without the hat. What is the plan now?"

"Take the byroads back to Finea, park the car there and lie low at my uncle's till the guards have finished rampaging round the countryside. After a few days, they'll have settled down."

"You really don't want me to get away from here."

Holland grinned boyishly. "Circumstances keep getting in the way, that's all."

At the next junction, Holland swung to the left and the car lurched over the uneven surface of a narrow road. The bends became sharper. Sabine suddenly clutched his arm.

"Stop! Stop the car!"

"But we're not far enough—"

He broke off: Sabine was holding her mouth. He pulled over to the side, and Sabine jumped out. She vomited over a bush on the incline of a ditch. Holland stayed inside the car, with the engine running, anxiously watching the mirror for pursuers. He handed out a handkerchief to Sabine and she wiped her mouth. She felt light-headed, relieved: she had expunged the worst of her fears, the image of the uniformed policeman dropping to the ground after Holland had struck him, the shots, the getaway. It did not seem to her to be a part of her life, or something she had actually seen. She climbed into the car again and Holland immediately put his foot down before she had even properly closed the door. With a screech, the car sped down the road.

20

They drove for half an hour. There were few road signs and Holland had only a hazy idea which direction they were driving in. He kept an anxious watch on the petrol gauge. Eventually they reached the main Oldcastle-Mountnugent road and he began to relax. Sabine, who had been silent and morose since she had thrown up, became talkative when they drove through Mountnugent. This cheered Holland, who had begun to wonder if he was taking her back against her will.

"Your uncle told me about your family," she said as they crossed the humped-back bridge that led away from the village. Holland kept his eyes fixed on the road. He knew now that there were no pursuers, but the guards up and down the country had probably been alerted, and the Wolseley would be easy to recognise. People stopped and looked at them. Some even waved.

"What family?"

"He told me your father died when you were a very small child, and then they sent you and your mother away from the farm so the next brother could take it over."

"There was no call to tell you all that."

"Does it hurt you, to talk about this?"

"It's all in the past. I don't know why FX has to keep dredging it all up." He was brusque, as though annoyed, but at some level it pleased him that Sabine had wanted this knowledge. It was a brutal story and

inspired pity. He was not just a gunman but a dispos-
sessed orphan.

"It's interesting. Your mother must have been bitter."

"She was. Anyway, what about you? You never told
me what your father does for a living."

"He's a doctor. But he was finding it impossible to
work under the new government."

"Did you have a boyfriend or anything like that back
in Germany?"

Sabine considered her response. "Yes, I was—how
does one say it—betrothed to be married."

"Ah," said Holland, as though she had explained
everything.

Sabine began to root around in her purse. "Look, I
have a picture of him. His name is Franz, a typical boring
German name." Artlessly she thrust a small photograph
into Holland's hand. He struggled with it, one thumb
holding it fast to the steering wheel. The picture showed
a young fair-haired man sitting on a rug. His features were
rather bland. Holland took an instant dislike to him: he
especially disliked the casual way his legs were splayed, and
the knowing smile.

He said: "So this is the boyfriend. I suppose he's waiting for you back in Berlin?"

Sabine took the picture from him and returned it to
her bag. She said with bitterness: "He's an Aryan, so getting married to me is forbidden. We tried to keep meeting
but it was impossible."

Holland felt genuinely sorry for her. "I didn't think
things were that bad."

Sabine remained quiet. In a sudden burst of blueness,
Lough Sheelin appeared briefly on their left. "Excuse
my ignorance, but what exactly is an Aryan when he's at
home?"

"You're an Aryan. All the Europeans are Aryans, more or less, but not the Jews."

"So it's like being a member of a club without knowing about it?"

"What about you, Mr Holland? Do you have a girlfriend hidden away in the hills?"

Holland coughed and gulped. "There was somebody, a journalist in *The Irish Press*. But nothing came of it."

Sabine put on her puzzled look. "Did you have a big argument?"

"No, it was just the usual Irish thing."

Sabine put on one of her exaggerated sarcastic smiles. "What is the usual Irish thing, Mr Holland?"

Holland ran his fingers through his hair. "My God, you always want everything spelled out, don't you?"

"Yes, I do."

"Well, she was a believer, do you know what I mean, a respectable, mass-going sort of girl."

"You mean, she would not have sexual relations with you?"

Holland's cheeks and ears reddened.

"You have a way with words, Sabine."

"Are all the girls so chaste here?"

They were on a relatively straight stretch of road. Holland turned to look at her, pointedly ignoring her question.

"What about you and Mr Right in the picture then?"

Sabine pursed her lips. "You know that religious Jews do not have sex before marriage either. It's the same."

"But you're not religious, unless you've been keeping very quiet about it. And if you were, you wouldn't have got yourself engaged to an Aryan."

Sabine hesitated. She hadn't intended the conversation to take this turn. Finally she said: "We loved each other, very much—*completely*—if you must know."

Silence filled the car. The clouds moved rapidly above them as though on a screen: the countryside appeared static by comparison. Holland felt punctured, empty of spirit. Sabine thought of Franz, the smell of his sweat after he'd played tennis, the weight of his muscles as his arm rested on her, the taste of his mouth, his voice, his gentleness.

They arrived at the place where Holland had previously hidden the car. He drove through the wall of greenery into the boreen, turned and parked behind the stand of bushes as before. They sat in silence listening to the gulls circling overhead. Holland tapped the petrol gauge before turning off the engine. The arrow had sunk to the bottom of the dial.

"It'll be best to wait here till dawn," he told Sabine. "We can take a boat out to FX's house and set it adrift."

"We are refugees from the law," Sabine said sadly.

"Yeah, fugitives," Holland corrected. He'd been a fugitive on and off for the last five years: all that he could judge this by was how hotly they were pursuing him.

"We have the food from your uncle."

They ate some of the soda bread and drank cold tea from the bottle. After they had eaten, Holland suggested they go down to the lakeshore. There were thick grey clouds gathering to the south over the wooded slopes of Mullaghmeen but they seemed to be suspended there and came no nearer. Holland and Sabine sat on the rocks and watched the pulsating aerial dance of the midges over the water. Intermittently the sun shone directly on the lake, peppering the surface with starbursts of jagged white light.

The sun grew brighter, the strange blanketing light of midsummer spread across the sky. Bees fumbled with the flowering clover growing in the shade of the trees. Sabine fell into a trance. The suffocating smell of the shore plants, the gentle rippling of the waters against the shore robbed her of all feeling. She could feel the land invading her, loosening her ties to the past.

Holland's thoughts were more specific. The lake waters put him in mind of the biblical stories his mother had once told him. As a child he had imagined Jesus on this inland sea, striding across the water as his followers cried in astonishment from their boat. And it struck him that Sabine too was a Jew. Of the same stock as Jesus, the apostles, Joseph and Mary.

Sabine lay down drowsily on some couch grass and pulled up her dress to expose her legs to the sun. She could hear Holland putting an extra round into the magazine of the Parabellum and checking the firing mechanism. He could just see Sabine's hair spread out on the grass.

"Your family," he said, "where did they come from originally?"

It took Sabine a few seconds to respond. "My father's family, who were called Cappadosa, came from Holland a hundred years ago. Before that they lived in Spain. They were Sephardic Jews. My mother's family, Bloch, came from near Poznan in Poland."

"But I mean, when did they come to Europe from Palestine?"

Sabine sat up and gave him one of her looks. Amused or sarcastic; Holland was not sure which. "Orwen, you know, that was a *very* long time ago. We don't have the train tickets any more."

Holland felt foolish, and rechecked the magazine of the gun.

"I look like my father's side of the family," Sabine continued. "Dark. My brother, though, is quite light. His hair is like yours." She looked critically at Holland's hair as though for the first time. "Perhaps a little darker," she said as if worried that she might be contradicted. Her thoughts turned to Germany. Her brother's looks might save him. He could pass for a German and get to Switzerland or head east. She imagined soldiers on guard at the border, searching for refugees. And then not wanting to think too much, she said she would like to go for a swim.

"A swim? We have to be careful; there might be fishermen on the lake."

"You don't have to worry. I can keep my underclothes on if that is what I must do." She was being deliberately naughty, *frisch*: for the first time she felt utterly safe with Holland.

He hopped onto one of the bigger rocks and scanned the lake. Visibility was good. They would be able to spot a rowing boat long before it could get close enough for anyone to see them. There was no reason why she should not go for a quick dip. Sabine stripped down to her bra and panties behind a nearby tree. She fetched a towel from one of her bags in the car, and picked her way delicately over the rocks to get to the water. Holland watched her progress, the gun forgotten by his side. She halted when the water was up to her knees and shivered violently. She hugged herself.

"This is certainly not the Wannsee."

"It's not the sea at all."

Sabine waded in to deeper water. She giggled at the cold. There was sand under her feet, so she flung herself headlong in, dived and surfaced ten yards away. She rinsed out the bad taste remaining in her mouth. It was exhilarating, extraordinary to have such a huge body of water to herself.

She shouted at Holland to join her. At first he declined but eventually the temptation was too much for him. He took off his shoes and socks, the heavy trousers, his jacket and shirt and waded in after her until the water reached his waist. Sabine popped up beside him as lithe and as natural in this element as an otter. Her wet hair was blue black in colour, and her eyes sparkled. Holland was also aware of her nipples, chestnut brown against the translucent fabric of her brassiere.

"Come on! Make a dive! Make a dive!" she ordered.

"Do we have towels?"

"Yes, yes, we have one: we can share it. Come on, dive! The water is good."

"I'm afraid I can't swim."

She grasped his hand. "It's not deep. Come."

He lost his balance, fell forward; and for a second he was underneath her, under the surface viewing her face. Inside him, for once, there was a sense of utter tranquillity and then he rose up, gasping for breath.

On the shore they shared the towel. When Sabine laughed out loud and tried to take the towel from him, he reeled her in and attempted to kiss her on the lips. Sabine smiled and turned her face away. It was a strange scene: they were both practically naked and yet there was an extraordinary shyness.

"I thought Republicans did not chase women: all that mattered was the Cause."

Her flippancy cooled him. "That sounds like one of FX's lines."

Sabine was suddenly serious. "He told me lots of things when you were away."

"Did he show you his collection of maps?"

She laughed. "Is it like his stamp collection? Does he invite all the girls up to see them?"

"He has ordnance survey maps of the whole area. He puts little 'x's beside the famine graves."

"Yes. I saw the maps in a cupboard in the kitchen. He showed me where there was a mass grave, beside the church. He said there were thousands of bodies thrown in, without coffins."

"And at the same time they were exporting food by the shipload from every port."

"The British?"

"Yes. Have you never wondered why the countryside here is so empty?"

Sabine touched the top of his arm.

"You're too white, Holland. You should get yourself brown in the sun."

Holland looked at Sabine's tanned skin. "I'm not like you. I'd only burn."

For an instant there was a peculiar intimacy between them, as though all secrecy had been blown away and they could say anything to each other. Their eyes met with a painful intensity. Sabine was the first to look away. She stood up and began to put on her clothes.

They got a few hours' sleep in the car before the dawn chorus woke Holland. He touched Sabine's shoulder and she opened her eyes to look directly into his.

They ate the last of the soda bread and struggled with their baggage along the bog road leading to Finea. There was no sign of FX's boat this time. Holland chose another one, an old unpainted wreck that he hoped no one would miss, and found the oars he had hidden behind a hedge on a previous occasion. The boat was leaky but Holland made good progress, even where it was choppy, farther out on the lake. Sabine bailed frantically all the way, terrified by the insidious intrusion of the water. Holland seemed surprisingly relaxed despite his inability to swim.

It was, she thought, as if he was suspicious of peace and only happy when there was an element of danger in his activities.

"I'll have to persuade FX to let us stay a few more days until the hunt dies down. Then we'll find some petrol for the car and get you away from here."

Sabine nodded, but barely looked up. Her muscles were aching from the effort of bailing water but the far edge of the lake was in sight.

They beached the boat, left their luggage in it and went up to the house. Outside the back door, they heard a strange wailing sound. Holland made a joke about FX holding a Halloween party. Sabine was too tired to respond. They walked into the kitchen. The sound they had heard was coming from the radio.

"That's strange. FX is usually very careful about switching off the wireless. The batteries must be nearly dead." He went over and turned it off. The house returned to silence and a kind of timelessness. Holland felt the presence of his mother, remembered the shape of her hand in his.

Sabine sank into the armchair by the fireplace. She said: "He must be still asleep upstairs. Shall we wake him?"

"It's early, but he's usually a light sleeper. It's strange he didn't hear us come in."

Holland felt the fire. It was quite cold. There were no embers. He took the Parabellum out of his knapsack.

"Stay here, Sabine. I'm going upstairs."

Sabine, too tired to be alarmed, waved her hand languidly from the chair.

Holland went through the motions, carefully opening the door to the hall, creeping along the wall with the Parabellum lowered, grasped in both hands with the safety off. But he did not feel the presence of danger. A fly stood motionless on a banister railing. The stillness of the house was almost physical; he could sense its yawning emptiness in his belly. The gun still lowered, he turned to go up the stairs. And it was there that he found FX.

He was lying at the foot of the stairs like a broken toy, arms and legs splayed and twisted. His eyes were open, glassily accusatory: it was a look Holland had never seen him express before, not even when he had upbraided him about the Parabellum.

As Caffrey once had shown him, he thrust his hand onto his neck, immediately under the jaw. But there was no need to check for something that his eyes told him wasn't there. The body was already cold and stiff, an object rather than a human being, the face set into a permanent mask. Whatever the poets or romantics might say, death resembled only itself.

He sighed and sank down beside him. It seemed that if he let people out of his sight, they died: they used this excuse to escape. Everyone around him had been rounded up—his father, his mother and now FX. In some other better world perhaps they were waiting for him. The air around him seemed suddenly populated. He could feel the power of the recent dead, wellsprings of memory so recent that he might have turned his head for a second and found himself staring into living eyes. A knocking sound above him brought him back to the present. He bounded up the stairs and methodically went through each room, gun at the ready. There was no sign that anyone else had been there, no sign of a struggle. The banging noise he had heard came from an open window in FX's bedroom. He fastened it and went down the stairs to tell Sabine what had happened. She was fast asleep in the armchair by the fireplace. He shook her gently awake, and told her that FX was dead.

It took her a few moments to understand what he was saying.

"He fell down the stairs?" she asked in disbelief. Holland's eyes, however, were impossible to misread.

"That's what it's supposed to look like." He tried not to imagine how it had happened. Perhaps his heart had simply given out when they were questioning him. They could hardly have expected him to know much more than their destination. They—and it must have been more than one—had probably thrown him down the stairs to make it look like an accidental death. Sabine still seemed shocked. Holland's hand rested casually on her shoulder. He was aware that she looked much more upset than him.

"What I'd like to know is how they managed to find out we were here."

Sabine head sank. "I'd like to see him."

"I don't know if that's a good idea." He noticed that she was wearing her determined look. "All right, do it if you want, then go down to the cottage and hide there till I get back."

"Where are you going?"

"I can't leave him here like this. The rats... I'm going up to the neighbours. They used to have Republican sympathies. I don't think they'll give me away and they can tell the cops that *they* found him."

He took one last look at FX's remains and left. Before going up the hill he checked the soft ground around the house and found the telltale thread of motorcar tyres at the bottom of the lane. A cigarette butt was sticking out from a tuft of grass. He picked it up and sniffed at it. Besides the smell of the tobacco, there was an additional herbal aroma he didn't recognise. The cigarette wasn't the usual Woodbine or Carroll's the locals smoked; it had the scent of a foreign brand, but one that filled him with a vague sense of familiarity.

In the kitchen of the neighbouring farm, Holland kept his suspicions to himself: he simply told the farmer and his wife that he had found FX dead at the bottom of the stairs. The woman blessed herself and said she would get one of her boys to fetch the priest.

"The guards will have to be informed too," the farmer said. He looked warily at Holland.

"I'd be obliged if you left me out of the story. You can tell them that I stayed with FX but don't mention that I was here recently."

"If I know them fellas, they'll want to talk to you anyway."

"That's their business. You won't be involved. I promise you."

The farmer nodded; his strong fingers meshed together like parts of a machine. "I'm giving nothing away," he said.

Holland returned to the house and filled a cardboard box with food. He also took FX's heavy gardening knife. In life he had loved it, and Holland did not want it to fall into the hands of strangers.

Sabine and Holland hid themselves as far away from the house as they could, on a small rise, and watched as first the priest arrived in his car, skidding to a halt in a hail of dust and gravel; then the doctor, also by car, but carefully, and finally the local guard, a broad, thick-set man on a stately black bicycle. A few neighbours made an appearance too, looking awkward, as though unsure whether FX might suddenly appear and ask them what they were doing on his property.

They sat and watched their comings and goings while eating some of the food from FX's kitchen. Holland felt removed from the complicated rituals of death which obtained in rural Ireland: the Movement had dealt in such matters more practically. The heroic dead were given rousing, pompous funerals with a speech and a volley; despised informers were hurriedly buried in shallow graves lost in a wood or in the side of a bog.

"I can't believe he's dead," he told Sabine. "Last time I spoke to him he was planning to grow tomatoes behind the house. He was going to get plate glass from a ruined house and build seed boxes. Now it's his house that's abandoned."

Sabine made no comment at first. She looked miserable. "I feel it is my fault. If you would not have taken me here, he would still be alive."

"If it's anyone's fault, it's mine," Holland said charitably. But his words did not console her. He could not feel any bitterness, not even toward those who had killed him. FX had been his only remaining anchor to his family's past. Without him, there appeared to be nothing tethering him directly to the world.

Sabine returned to the cottage while Holland kept a watch on the house. The priest and doctor soon left. A couple of middle-aged women came by on foot, presumably to help lay out the body. Holland wondered if they would hold a wake. Above the horizon, thick clouds bunched together, black and blue, like bruised fists. The hours passed. The guard's bicycle stayed where he had left it, propped up against the wall below the kitchen window. Smoke wafted out of the chimney. The sight of it filled Holland with hate. What right had these people to misuse the possessions of the recently dead? And it pained him too that the policeman hadn't gone. Late in the afternoon, a ramshackle ambulance arrived. Sabine was lying beside Holland when this happened, she had just brought him some sandwiches. Holland stopped chewing and stared intently at the house as two attendants carried out FX's remains in a stretcher.

"This isn't good. It looks like they're taking him away to open him up."

"What does it mean?"

"It could mean they suspect foul play."

Holland sent Sabine back to clear the cottage so they could make a quick getaway into the woods farther along the shore. A car arrived half-an-hour after the ambulance had left. Inside were four men, two uniformed Gardaí, and two plain-clothes detectives. The guard who had arrived by bicycle came out of the house to meet them. His hand pointed vaguely in the direction of the lake and Holland felt a wave of unease ride through his stomach. He crept back to the cottage, helped Sabine to get their belongings out, and then they retreated into the thick vegetation along the shore. It began to drizzle.

Far away from the cottage they rested and took stock. They had enough food for three days, four if they were frugal. After that, Holland reckoned he would be able to sneak back to the house and collect more. At the very least he could dig up vegetables from FX's garden. There were plenty of potatoes still in the earth.

Using FX's heavy gardening knife, Holland began to construct a rough shelter out of branches and bracken, camouflaging its outline with handfuls of grass. The maxim they had been taught in training camp came back to him, with the strong Kerry accent intact: *when it is hidden, make even its hiding hidden.*

As soon as the shelter was ready, Sabine placed their provisions and bags in a corner and crept inside. Wild birds cackled and shrieked from the lake. Holland imagined the police combing the shoreline and finding the boat they had borrowed in Finea. The wind picked up and tugged absentmindedly at their primitive dwelling. The human world, the world of civilisation, seemed far away.

Sabine thought of her family in Germany, the large apartment they had shared before the new government had come to power. She wondered what she had done to deserve such suffering. Why were they being hunted like wild animals? Why had she been sent to live like this in the wilderness? She remembered the opening line of a Sephardic poem her father had taught her, *My heart is in the east, and I in the uttermost west* and felt keenly the oceanic sadness and self-pity of exile. She began to cry softly, her sobs blending with the light beat of the rain against the leaves. Holland put his arms around her and their faces, salty with rain and sweat and fear, met for an instant. At first Sabine shied away, but Holland overcame her reluctance and drew her to him. They kissed and lay together silently as the rain beat time above them.

And then there was the voice. A voice, that seemed no more than yards away from them, cracked through the shelter like a pistol shot: they were certain that they had been discovered. Holland's hand found the curved butt of the Parabellum, even though he wondered whether an escape was feasible. How could they break through a cordon of five police? He looked out from the shelter and saw a man wearing a heavy Garda greatcoat standing on a small headland twenty yards away. The guard shouted again and waved an arm as a sign to a colleague, somewhere to his right. Holland thought that the signal meant that the police were moving in on them, that they had seen the shelter. But the guard suddenly turned around and walked back towards the house. The rain had probably put them off a more detailed search: either that or they had simply given up, not really believing that anyone would be foolish enough to hide where they were hiding. Sabine was kneeling beside him, holding his left hand. Her finger could feel the seconds reverberating inside Holland's wristwatch; unbearable seconds that mimicked his heartbeat. How could Holland remain unmoved? Her own pulse was racing. Minutes went by and there was no sign of pursuit. They heard a man's voice, distorted by successive echoes, booming across the water. The disconnected vowels and consonants became fewer and fainter and finally stopped; then came a profound, welcoming silence.

The rain fell automatically for a long while, the sound of it striking the leaves like an engine idling. Sabine felt tears well up again. Holland held her gently and asked her what was wrong.

"It was the picture I showed you."

"The picture of your young fella in Germany?"

"Yes. I was remembering the last time we met."

Holland did not really want to hear more but he smiled sympathetically and moved himself into a more comfortable position beside her. He wrapped the Parabellum in some oilcloth.

"You can tell me about it, if it would help."

"It was in a café in Berlin, Café Schottenhaml. I walked up Siegesallee. I remember every step because I knew what was to happen. I had guessed it."

"He was waiting for you?"

"Yes. In the corner, as far away from the door as you can be. He must have come very early. He was already sitting with a coffee and a cognac and I remember seeing two cigarettes in the ashtray. He did not drink usually. The cognac was to give him courage."

She turned away: shadows grew out of the angles of her face. Her eyes narrowed with their sudden burden of tears. He had never seen an expression anything like this on her face before. Sabine could not say anything for a moment. Holland still had a clean handkerchief in his jacket pocket. He handed it to her. She wiped her eyes and blew her nose.

"He said he wanted to leave you?"

Sabine gulped and controlled her face enough to continue. "He said he loved me but that it was impossible with us. Impossible because I was a Jew." She stopped and her eyes stared unseeing into the rain before she continued. "And then he looked around him: he looked around, you understand, with *fear*, as though someone might hear what he had said. That look in his eyes, I cannot...."

Sabine broke down and sobbed against Holland's shoulder. He was perceptive enough to realise that this memory had worked its way inside Sabine like a poison. Perhaps, he thought, it was this image of the cold young man staring around him in a café, ashamed to be seen with her, that had propelled her out of Germany and brought her to Ireland.

When, towards evening, the rain eventually eased off, they went outside and added some branches to their shelter. Then they ate some food. Holland took his gun and crept back to the house. There were lights on in the kitchen but the police car was gone, as was the guard's black bicycle. He went back to Sabine, who was sorting through her clothes.

"We'll have to spend the night here."

Sabine looked shocked, as though the thought had never occurred to her.

"In the morning we can find something better. For the time being, we'll stay here. If anyone approaches, the best place to hide is in the red bog."

Sabine looked dubiously at the raised bog that stretched away towards the hills of Mullaghmeen. Between it and the lake were trees—alder, willow and sallow—and a great swathe of yellow reeds and bulrushes. She had grown accustomed to the countryside since moving into the lakeside cottage, but this was something else.

"I want to get out of here," she said slowly.

"We need to stay low, for the moment, Sabine. To get to the car, we'll have to go past the barracks in Finea and, even if we make it, we have no petrol. We'd get no more than a mile or two. They're looking for us. They know what kind of car we have."

"How long do you think we'll have to stay here?"

"A couple of days. We'll have to get FX's boat. Either that or try to walk along the shore to Finea and cross the Inny. We'd have to do it at night and that would be dangerous on foot. Some of the swamps here could swallow up a horse."

"It's bad. Everything is bad."

"It's good too. It means they can't make a proper sweep of the area. Unless they send in the army. They can only approach us from this side." He pointed towards FX's house.

"The army? Would they send in the army?"

"No, not unless they think we're Republicans. I don't think they'll connect us to the Oldcastle raid."

"But if they find the car?"

Holland was silent. He could picture them finding the car and not only connecting them to the Oldcastle raid but also to Farkas' disappearance. The odds were beginning to stack up against them.

"This is my plan," he said. "We wait a couple of days, then take FX's boat to Finea in the middle of the night. There is a petrol can and a rubber tube in FX's house. I can get hold of it before we take the boat."

"And the petrol?"

"There must be something motorised in Finea. If there isn't, we can take the car anyway and hope for the best."

"If all goes well, if this plans succeeds, then what? Where do we travel to?"

"The Six Counties, as we'd planned. You can take the ferry to Glasgow from Derry, and then the train to London."

"I've no proper papers. I'm an illegal alien."

"You won't need any papers if you travel from the Six Counties to Scotland. You have just been on holiday in Donegal if anyone asks." He said this in a resigned tone of voice, as though her departure was already inevitable.

"And you, Orwen, what is your plan for yourself?"

Holland's brow furrowed. "I can find my way back to Dublin and settle things with my associates."

"Your associates! How do they react to someone who does not obey orders? A bullet in the head; that is what I have heard."

Holland, angry, turned his head away. "It's not like that. I might face a reprimand, even a court martial. But I have done nothing to compromise the Movement; besides talking too much to you, that is."

He got up and left. Sabine felt an instant pang of sorrow and loneliness. She went outside but Holland was already gone. She observed the darkening Irish sky. The sun had disappeared and the remaining light had begun to decant towards the horizon, the clouds fading away like receding mountain ranges.

Sabine felt unclean and went down to the water's edge where it was clear of reeds, pulled up her skirt and hunkered down. Tiny lurid creatures swam and crawled in the mud and between the fronds. Her hands sank into the water and drew up enough to splash her face and ears. The water was like light made tangible. She splashed it on her hair, under her clothes, under her armpits. A flight of birds moved across the lake, silhouetted against the sky. Her fingers found seeds clinging to her clothes and to her hair. She stared at her hands as the eerie evening light played on the water covering them.

How could the world have changed so much? Here she was, on the run from the police, in the deserted centre of a country she had barely heard of six months ago. Her only protector was a gunman, a political fanatic, fighting for a cause she did not remotely understand. He seemed to be in love with her. If she died in this place, if they buried her here, her family would never be told about it. And she could so easily be killed. The people pursuing them were ruthless; she felt it, her body felt it.

She looked at her hands and watched them shake. A strange power went through her, a wave of energy. Her spine tingled as though flooded with warmth. The voices in her head, urging caution and obedience, suddenly became muted. Once again she saw Holland outside the car, the gun poised. She watched as the huge body of the sergeant collapsed on the road and saw Holland running pell-mell towards the armed detective, knowingly running towards a kind of death. Holland was prepared to die, said a new voice; he tempts fate and that is what makes him strong. Perhaps he really was a barbarian but then again these were barbarous times. Where would all her culture and learning lead her during these days of despair? Nowhere at all, in this wilderness. And yet Holland thrived here and drew strength from the land. She too could make use of the countryside if only she could overcome her fear. The words of Yehuda Halevi's poem came back to her, each phrase discernible, a cry of despair from an exile living in Spain 800 years ago:

My heart is in the east, and I in the uttermost west—
How can I find savour in food? How shall it be sweet to me?
How shall I render my vows and my bonds, while yet
Zion lieth beneath the fetter of Edom, and I in Arab chains?

21

Night fell, and Holland returned. He had been spying on the house which he now assured Sabine was deserted. With him he had a large pot, two tin plates and some cutlery. The remaining food had been stolen by the neighbours.

"All the pipe tobacco is gone too," he told Sabine. This was a great disappointment: his own supplies had run out long ago and he had had no opportunity to buy more tobacco in Oldcastle.

"What about the vegetables in the garden?"

"We could dig up spuds, I suppose, and collect a few vegetables. But people will notice if the earth is disturbed."

Sabine's hunger made her creative. "They'll say there are ghosts. Country people always believe in spirits, don't they?"

Holland shrugged. He doubted whether the people looking for them would be quite so superstitious, but on the other hand some part of him desired a final confrontation.

Sabine emptied one of her bags of clothes and followed Holland back to the house. He fetched the Tilley lamp from the byre and this bathed the garden in an eerie yellow light, which contrasted with the deep black of the trees and hedges around them. FX's spade protruded from the ground in the centre of the garden, exactly as he had left it. Holland walked over, wrenched it out of the earth and began to dig under the nearest potato plant. The blade sank easily into the soft earth and potatoes began to emerge from the soil in white clusters, skull-like under the light of the lamp. Sabine opened the bag and began to fill it but she couldn't keep her eyes off the house which loomed up in the background, its windows menacingly blind. To distract herself, she began to talk.

"Holland, why do you stay here with me? You could escape on your own. It would be much easier."

Holland grunted with the effort of pulling up the stalks. "How far would I get? As soon as they had you, they would come after me. Anyway, I promised Farkas that I'd look after you if anything happened to him."

"Farkas is either dead or he has disappeared of his own free will. He doesn't pay your wages any more. You do not actually owe him anything."

Holland stopped digging and looked at Sabine. The Tilley lamp hissed like a serpent in the background. It was easier to talk about this in the dark but, even so, Holland hesitated.

"This has nothing to do with money."

"It's me, isn't it?"

"I promised I'd look after you," repeated Holland, his breath short. "We'd better keep our voices down. The neighbours—"

"The nearest neighbours live about a kilometre away. Why don't you say what you feel? I'll understand."

"Is this not a dangerous conversation; for you I mean?" Even in the darkness Sabine could sense Holland's apprehension.

"How could it be dangerous for me? You could do whatever you wanted to me. Remember, you are the big strong man. I've seen what you can do."

"Well, you must be terrified then?"

"I trust you, Holland. So we can, at least, clean the—" Sabine hesitated, unsure of the right word.

"Clean the slate? Clear the air?"

"Yes."

Holland forgot about the potatoes, the digging. He even forgot how hungry he was. "What if I told you," he said, his voice wavering and atonal, "that I was fond of you?"

"It would not come as a surprise. I've seen how you look at me. It is better to be honest."

"Well, I suppose you'd have to say I love you then," said Holland, looking down at the potato drills.

Sabine hadn't expected him to say *that*. What could one reply? She looked up and said: "I will be honest too then. I don't think there is any future for us. We can be friends perhaps. We *are* friends. You're risking your life for me, but I cannot promise anything in return."

Holland felt lost; she had encouraged him to make a declaration, and then without ceremony had shot it down. He stuck the spade back into the earth. It swayed as though momentarily alive.

He said: "It's dangerous to stay here. We'd better get back with these spuds. I'll see if there's any salt up at the house."

Holland walked off without looking at her. Sabine was not indifferent to the pain she had caused. In fact, with the strange light, the enclosed intimacy of the garden, its colony of vegetables, silent and in repose, she felt she had experienced Holland's feeling of rejection directly, like an electric shock passed from one person's hand to another's. She stared at the potatoes and bent down to gather the last one into the bag. It was about the same size as—and, rubbed clean, as smooth as—an apple, and the yellow light gave it a fruity pinkish hue. Only in her hands did it turn bone white.

That night Holland took them as far along the shore as he could get, close to where the river Inny left the lake. He built up a fire in the hearth of a ruined cottage in the middle of a ring fort. The stone walls of the cottage shielded the light of the fire from most angles and there was sufficient updraught in the chimney to draw the smoke skyward into the night air.

Holland rinsed the potatoes in the river, near its mouth, and covered them with water in the pot. When they were nearly ready, he opened a tin of corned beef and let it heat on a stone placed in the fire. The smell was intoxicating. They burnt themselves in their hurry to extract the potatoes, their fingers stumbling and distant in the flickering light and startling shadows thrown up by the fire. Holland brought out the salt and a small slab of butter he had saved from FX's kitchen. The butter melted quickly. He ate the potatoes whole, as he had seen them do in the west of Ireland: Sabine meticulously peeled hers. The corned beef tasted like the finest steak, and they washed their meal down with tea from the kettle he had taken.

After they had eaten, they sat at the entrance to the cottage and watched the lake, so black and still below them that they expected to see stars in it. Water birds called to each other from the reed beds, their furtive lives continuing under cover of darkness. But there were no stars and no wind. The invisible clouds were fastened over their heads as tight as a lid.

There was only one indication of human settlement. Across the lake, on a dark hillside, they could discern a feeble spasm of light. A kitchen lamp probably, thought Holland, a farmer and his wife worrying over their accounts or an old bachelor reading a copy of the parish magazine. Holland could imagine the oak chairs, a dresser full of blue delft, and a pool of yellow light on the oil-cloth. He imagined himself with such people in such a house: calves fed and warm in the byre, machinery rusting in the corner of the yard, the smell of milk and grain and dung intermingling, and all around them the eternal fields resting under the stars till dawn. A cliché, he knew, the romantic world of the farmer, and just as impossible a goal for him as studying at a university or even getting a normal job.

Sabine sat in silence across from him. Her hair was blacker than any part of the night. She was thinking of a picture from the Munch exhibition she had gone to see in London before travelling to Dublin. The ring fort, the ruined cottage, the morbid colours of the lake and an IRA gunman sitting beside her, all blended into a single canvas.

22

Holland and Sabine slept together in the shelter. It was cold and they kept all their clothes on. Sabine wore an extra jumper and slacks but even that wasn't enough. During the coldest part of the night, when the wind freshened, she crept over to Holland and pressed herself tight against his back for warmth. Holland pretended he was still asleep, and kept his breathing regular. Her slender arm moved across his chest. Her heat seeped into him and eased the pain of rejection. In sleep, she pressed so hard against him that he found his face pushed up against the cold, inert blackness of the Parabellum.

The next morning while they were breakfasting on the remaining boiled potatoes, Sabine said something disparaging about Irish culture.

"We have the oldest literature in Western Europe," Holland said defensively.

"I don't mean all that. I mean *high* culture: classical music, painting, modern novelists, poets. What there is that I have seen is all Anglo-Irish—and there's not much of that."

Holland could hear Mrs Fitzgibbons' superior tones in Sabine's voice. "There's traditional music, storytellers, old songs—"

"Yes, yes, but this is all what one calls in German part of the wild culture, not the garden culture that is cultivated."

"What the hell is that supposed to mean?"

Sabine was surprised that he had used a swearword, but she carried on regardless. "The garden cultures, the cultivated nations, are the ones that had major courts— the French, the English, the Italians, the Spanish."

Holland felt a bubble of indignation growing inside him. "But how could the Irish…? The English kept us down for centuries, like slaves until we rose up."

Sabine looked at him sympathetically, which made him feel worse. She nibbled delicately at the potato in her hand.

"Just a few miles away," continued Holland, sounding ever more desperate, "Owen Roe trained his men and then marched against three English armies with superior weapons and training. And Maeve's army from Connacht passed through right here where we're standing."

"Who won?"

"Who won what?"

"This Maeve army or this Owen army; who won the war?"

Holland recognised defeat. "There were sixteen hundred years between both events. What I'm trying to say is that our ancestors fought for Irish culture, an ancient culture. How can you compare it to a garden?"

"Your own leader, Mr Byrne senior—"

"We do overuse the name a little," conceded Holland, who had forgotten McDaid's alias.

"—well, he said you were plant bleeders, isn't that so?"

"*Breeders*. Plant breeders," corrected Holland wearily. He felt he had lost the run of this conversation long ago.

"I've made my point."

"Have you ever been to the National Museum in Dublin? Have you see all the Celtic stuff there? There was nothing like that in the rest of Europe at the time."

"Apart from Italy and Greece. And did you know, the man who runs the museum, Dr Adolf Mahr, is a Nazi? The Irish had to appoint an Austrian Nazi to look after their culture."

Holland ignored her remark and said: "Maybe the Jews should have concentrated a bit more on fighting and dropped some of the culture."

"Perhaps," Sabine said enigmatically. Her eyes were suddenly distant, scanning the lakeshore. Holland was worried that he had offended her but she turned back to him and smiled.

"I'll teach you to swim," she announced. "All soldiers have to be able to swim."

"It's too dangerous: we'd be seen."

"Are you scared? There's a place there where the river comes out. The reeds will hide us."

They walked down to the shoreline and stripped to their underclothes. Holland left the Parabellum beside a rock. He was being foolish, he knew. If anyone came, they would be defenceless but he couldn't resist Sabine's enthusiasm. They went into the water. First there was mud, then sand. At the mouth of the Inny, the water soon reached up to Holland's belly. Sabine dived and popped up beside him. Her face was very close. Droplets of water, like pearls, clung to her dark eyelashes. In the distance, across the expansive surface of the lake, the fields along the shore seemed to belong to another continent.

Sabine asked him to try to dive. He launched himself into the water, not caring, and she caught him as he thrashed with his arms.

"Use your legs," she urged. He told his legs to splash up and down. Water sprayed over Sabine. She flicked her head, her wet curls almost flat against her scalp, still holding him. But her left hand lost its grip and she touched

197

a part of him lower down, which produced an immediate reaction. He's like a wild horse, she thought. They collapsed laughing, spluttering, and Sabine disappeared under the water to swim back to the shore. Holland, released from his fear, threw his arms forward and dived, his legs churning the water behind him like a steamboat. He caught Sabine near the reed bed on the muddy foreshore and pinned her down in the shallow water. He opened his eyes. He was jammed up against her breast, his mouth pressed against her throat. Her eyes were wild, and at the same time, shy.

"You would not," she said.

"What?"

Sabine could feel the mud sucking at her toes, oozing along her back. Neither of them could move.

"We could change lessons," suggested Holland, short of breath. "German, instead of swimming. You promised once."

"What? I can't move."

"Parts of the body. What's this?" His finger ran down her face.

"*Jochbein, die Wange,*" she said automatically.

"*Und das?*"

"*Die Nase.*"

He ran his fingers along her upper lip, the flushed pink skin contrasting with the grey-green water of Kinale.

"*Der Mund.*"

"Ah, masculine, and this?" He stroked her neck.

"*Hals, der Hals, hör auf!*"

"*Und hier?*"

"*Der Schulter.*"

"Like, 'shoulder', very interesting."

"Yes, and, Holland, I've had enough of this!"

But her eyes were still wild and saying something else.

198

Holland placed his forefinger gently on her right nipple, which protruded deep brown beneath the delicate material of her bra.

"You wouldn't dare," she exclaimed rather inconsequently, because he already had.

Sabine's eyes stared up at him like those of a beautiful wild animal, a deer trapped by the hunter.

From the reed bed close by came the high tremulous wail of a coot.

"*Hier?*" inquired Holland.

"*Bauch. Es reicht!*"

His hand slid into the top of her panties and caressed the damp pubic hairs.

Sabine's breath was coming in quick gulps.

"*Schambein. Jetzt reicht's.* Enough!"

Sabine was both raging and aroused.

"I'll stop if you let me kiss you," Holland said.

"One kiss," said Sabine, between a laugh and a shout. Every millimetre of her skin had become tremendously sensitive. Even the mud seemed to be teasing her with an unbearable tenderness.

Holland moved in over her. His lips touched hers as gently as the wing of a moth. And then the kiss: they lunged at each other like hungry birds of prey. The mud squelched as their bodies slid and ground hard against each other, locking them into their bed of mud.

During the first kiss, which did not ever properly stop, Holland's fingers stroked Sabine between the legs and sank softly into her. He played with her until she felt she would explode. Slowly, gently, she began to caress his penis. He entered her, briefly, no more than three or four thrusts, the last one deep, making her body want to hold onto him. Then he withdrew. She eased the foreskin up and down until Holland could hold out no more and his seed spilled over her belly and into the lake waters. An eerie light, ancient but benign, flooded into Holland's head.

They floundered ashore like survivors of a shipwreck.

Afterwards, Sabine was still in a kind of rage, although Holland couldn't figure out if she was angry with him or with herself. "This should never have happened," she told him as they washed the mud from their skin and clothes. Holland nodded, unconvinced, not feeling the least guilty. Even though he knew it might never happen again, he felt supremely happy.

Sabine spent the rest of the day washing her underclothes, collecting firewood and improving the shelter. Holland returned to the house, caught and killed one of FX's hens and collected carrots and onions from the garden. He brought the food back to the ruined cottage, plucked and gutted the hen, and set it over the fire to boil with the vegetables. When they had eaten, Holland took down the old shelter and began to build a new camp in a more secluded spot between Kinale's tiny sister lake, Lough Darragh, and Kinale itself. It was the ideal place, with the red bog and great walls of briar behind them, birch, willow and sallow trees on either side and the dense reed beds in front. They constructed a new shelter and Holland dug a latrine using the spade from FX's garden while Sabine built a fireplace with rocks from the lake's edge.

That night Sabine crept over to him again and stretched her arm over his chest. He turned around, very slowly, until he was facing her. In the pitch-black interior of the shelter they explored each other's faces, and slowly their hands wandered farther down. They made love again, this time with the methodical ease of people who know each other well.

When they had finished, they put on their clothes and sat beside the dying embers of their fire. It was a night so large and complete with stars that the earth disappeared beneath one's feet.

"Why do the stars twinkle, do you think?" Holland asked.

"They say it is all distortion. Everything is distorted: as though we are looking at coins at the bottom of a pond. What are the stars to you?"

Holland looked at her and smiled: "Bullet holes, thousands and thousands of bullet holes."

"And the moon?"

It was the middle of summer and the moon was a semi-circle, growing fatter each night.

"It's a big exit wound. Boom, somebody shot right through the universe."

They laughed. He noticed her small even teeth.

"You're a primitive!" she said.

"Yes, I'm a simple-minded Paddy, with a bunch of reflexes instead of a brain."

"Your reflexes have saved us up to now."

23

A week passed by. They refused to speak of the future. The weather remained good with only occasional showers. During daylight hours they swam in the secluded coves or gathered firewood. Sometimes they startled the wild goats that lived on the other side of the bog and once they saw a family of otters gambolling in the river. In the evenings Sabine taught Holland German words or talked about Berlin. Holland made a fishing rod and taught Sabine to fish. At night they made love.

As the days passed, Holland wondered at the changes in Sabine. This new Sabine learned to enjoy the fresh air, the perennial greenness, as though the big-city world she had grown up with had only had a superficial influence. Her skin became radiant, her eyes grew milder and her body became supple and strong. They talked about almost everything and managed to avoid the subjects where their opinions differed. Holland was happy, even though he knew it couldn't last. Food was getting harder to find. FX's hens had disappeared and even the potatoes in the garden were running out. Weeds were already pushing up little islands of greenery in the loose topsoil.

"Why's the river called the Inny?" Sabine asked one morning just as they had finished a particularly spartan breakfast.

"It's probably from *abhainn*, the Irish word for river."

"Hitler was born beside a river called the Inn."

"Were there Celts down there too?"

"I don't know. I'm not really sure who the Celts were."

"I don't think anyone is. According to the books, they seem to have been everywhere before they settled down here." He threw a leaf into the water. "You know, they say that if you spit into the Inny, it takes a hundred years before the spit reaches the sea."

Sabine said coquettishly: "Let us see who can spit the farthest."

But before she could move, Holland grabbed her arm. "Wait a second," he whispered, and pointed to an object on the lake.

They crept behind a reed bed farther along the shore to watch.

The boat bobbed gently, adrift it seemed, until they noticed the single occupant, a young man in a tweed suit and a broad-rimmed trilby. He didn't look like a local; indeed, he didn't even look like a proper fisherman. For one thing, he made no attempt to use the fishing tackle at the stern. Instead he scrutinised the shoreline on either side as though attempting to peer through the reed beds and dense foliage of the trees.

The wind was strong on the lake and at one point whipped the hat off his head. It got caught on his fishing accoutrements and flapped about there like a demented bird unable to alight. The man scrambled after it, caught it, and pulled it back on his head.

Holland looked at Sabine and smiled grimly: "I think I know who that is."

Sabine held his arm: "So it isn't a local man?"

"No."

"He isn't very interested in catching anything. He hasn't touched the fishing equipment."

"Well, he's more a fisher of men than of fish."

"Are we the ones he's after?"

"I would be very surprised if he wasn't."

Holland extracted the Parabellum and took off the safety catch. Sabine examined his face. It wore a sunny smile as though he were about to shoot tin ducks in the fairground.

"Could you hit him from this far?"

"I might be able to sink his boat from here. And that would do it: he can't swim an inch."

"You're not really going to shoot him, are you? He hasn't even seen us." She could feel a strange tension inside her; to witness Holland do this would be a horror, but it would be striking back at an enemy who up till now had remained unseen. By proxy, she felt that she too had gained some power over life and death.

She grasped Holland's arm. "I forbid you to shoot."

Holland ignored her, aimed the pistol high and fired a single shot. Birds tore into the air all around them as though the landscape itself was breaking up. The fisherman responded immediately. He gathered up the oars and laboriously began to steer the boat towards them.

When he was about halfway, Sabine asked: "Shall I stay here too?" She had recognised Caffrey, but this hadn't made her feel less nervous.

"I'll talk to him. There's a chance he'll help us to get away from here. You'd better go back, hide yourself. I'll call you when he's gone."

"Perhaps he's here to kill you."

"It's hard to know what his orders might be. But he wouldn't parade around on the lake if he was going to plug me. And he wouldn't come on his own."

"How do you know he's alone?"

"There's nobody else on the lake. There's nothing but bog and forest behind us."

Sabine moved stealthily backwards through the trees and hid herself in the heather that grew on the raised bog like thick wiry hair.

Caffrey beached the boat awkwardly, fumbled with the mooring rope until finally tying it clumsily to one of the larger stones. He took a basket from the stern and jumped onto a flat rock where he balanced precariously before wading ashore. Holland couldn't see any sign of a weapon, although he knew his friend could easily have stowed a small revolver somewhere. Caffrey began to walk along a narrow path that the wild goats had made, and through a stand of willow trees. Holland moved in behind him and thrust the Parabellum into the small of his back.

"Caff, you're never going to win any prizes mooring a boat like that."

"You're not going to plug me before I reply to that insult, are you?"

"Just turn around slowly and put the basket on the ground."

Caffrey obeyed, and Holland sat down on a nearby rock cradling the Parabellum.

"Now take off the jacket and turn it inside out."

Caffrey stretched his arms wide, incredulous. "It's me for Christ's sake—your old friend. Believe me, I'm not armed. And even if I was, I wouldn't pull a gun on you."

Holland smiled. "Just humour me."

Caffrey did as he was asked. Holland was surprised by the quality of his clothes, as well as all the fishing equipment he had presumably hired. The IRA would never pay for anything as elaborate as this if it were simply a matter of executing a traitor. And they would hardly send out someone like Caffrey to a remote rural area when there were plenty of local volunteers who knew the terrain.

"Let me show you what I've got in the basket."

"It wouldn't be a Tommy gun, I suppose."

"No, just a couple of Mills bombs. I heard it was a good way of catching trout. I'll open it slowly."

Holland narrowed his eyes and yawned. He was having a hard time treating Caffrey as a potential assassin, but he felt protective towards Sabine.

Caffrey piled the contents of the basket onto the grass. Out came a loaf of bread, half a dozen tins of meat and vegetables, a jar of strawberry jam, some cold meats and two large slabs of cheese and butter. Lastly, like the finale of a conjuring trick, he pulled out a brown paper bag that burst in his hands, spilling bright red apples on the grass.

Holland could feel his mouth watering but he kept his eyes on Caffrey.

"You fishermen have good appetites."

"I thought ye might be a bit hungry."

Holland ignored the implication of 'ye' and said. "A fox gone to earth gets very hungry. That's a well-known fact. By the way, did the boys who raided Oldcastle get away all right?"

"The Dundalk unit? Yeah, they all made it home. They pulled in over £700. They were very lucky though. The detectives got stopped by a gangster on the loose with his moll in the front seat. So the cops and the army ended up haring round the wrong part of the country for the best part of a week."

Holland laughed. "I won't get any medals for it but I'm glad they got away."

"Let me sit down."

"Pull up one of them rocks."

Caffrey looked seriously at his companion as he perched himself on a stone. "No one's interested in getting you, Holland."

"That's not the way I look at it. You weren't one of the ones who visited my uncle?"

"I didn't even know you had an uncle, besides the ones you don't talk to."

Holland thought he knew Caffrey well enough to know he was telling him the truth.

"He's dead. I think the Mundial people did it, looking for us."

"I'm sorry to hear that. I swear I knew nothing about it. But I wouldn't put it past them." Caffrey paused to look directly at Holland. "How did things ever get this far, Holly?"

"I don't know. I just did the right thing by my lights. I took on a job I didn't want, when McDaid asked me. I protected Farkas when I had to and now all I'm trying to do is look after, well, the rest of my responsibilities." His voice dropped. "My own private business."

Caffrey tugged at his fair hair. "You're talking hairy fuckin' shite now, Holly. *We're* not supposed to have any private business." He looked around, scanning the thick vegetation. "So she *is* here? Probably about ten yards away hiding in the bushes. And you're the little Mammy bird chasing away all the hungry foxes."

"This can do a bit more damage than a beak," said Holland resting the Parabellum on his knee. "Anyway, you knew she was here. You hardly bought a fancy get-up like that and came all this way just to look for me."

"Oh don't underestimate your attractions. I've been doing my best to help you."

"Go on."

"There's a way out of this situation for everyone. The Mundial people think that the girl has some important papers. Either that or she knows where Farkas is."

"How could they know that? And what difference does it make to you? Isn't this our business? McDaid and the money. The Movement."

"The way you've been acting, everyone thinks you know something. Anyway, I'm wearing my Mundial hat for the moment."

"Since when have you been working for them?" asked Holland.

"Since McDaid told me to, and that's even before you joined them."

"So that's the way of it. You know more than you're letting on."

Caffrey sighed. "I know that the Movement is in trouble. They're talking about sending a bunch of raw lads straight to England after training in Killiney. They'll stand out a mile: country boys with serge suits and fighting caps. It's cynical, bloody-minded, and it won't work."

"You took the oath. You always have to obey orders: that's what you're always yapping on about to me."

For the first time in the conversation, Caffrey looked genuinely troubled.

"Forget all that. There's no crossover on this, Holly. I'm serving both sides. What I've been told to say is that they'll be waiting in Abbeylara beside the ruins tomorrow at dawn. Bring the girl along and the papers and there'll be no questions asked. They've agreed to give you £500 compensation. If you want, you can hand over the money to McDaid and square things with him."

"Why would they want Sabine if they have the papers?"

"They can use her to get Farkas. It's him they're really after. He's still alive—that's all they know."

"But why her?"

"You mean, you don't know?"

"Know what?"

"She's family; Farkas' niece. He won't let anything happen to her."

Somehow the shock of this revelation came as a relief. For a second he had expected Caffrey to say that Sabine was Farkas' mistress.

"One thing I don't understand is: why do the Mundial people want to hand over a whole lot of money to McDaid?"

"It's better for you not to know, believe me."

"Well, if I'm going to hand over Sabine, I might as well know why."

Caffrey looked uneasily over his shoulder, although it was unlikely that anyone other than Sabine was within a mile's radius of where they were sitting.

"The Movement and Mundial have the same interests: bringing down the British Empire. Mundial is really just a front for the Abwehr, the German secret service. Farkas started it but the Germans managed to get him to work for them. His connections in Germany allow the Jews to magically move their money out of the country, and the Abwehr control this for their own purposes. We got our cut, and the promise of more arms and ammunition. It was a fair deal all round."

"But what are we doing for them besides protecting Mundial."

"That's the thing. We give them information, which is really what they're about. You see, the Brits have lots of technical gimcracks the Germans want to develop too. They have this device that can spot aircraft from a distance so it can be shot down."

"A kind of ray gun?"

Caffrey smiled. "It's not from an episode of Buck Rogers. It's more like giant eye. They've built these towers along the coast, and they send out a beam that can see through cloud—day or night—for a hundred miles."

"So this is what you've been doing all this time in England, collecting information."

"The Germans are hopeless at it, total amateurs. I can pass for a native. I just put on a la-di-da accent, buy the right people a gin and tonic and they tell me everything."

"Have you forgotten they're fucking fascists, Caff. You're working for German fascists."

"I'm just obeying orders. People at the top of the Movement are happy for us to work with the Nazis."

"What about Mincey and the others in Spain fighting these fuckers?"

"Mincey's dead. I was going to tell you. A lot of them have handed in their guns over there, Holly. Nineteen in Jarama alone. They're getting butchered for nothing. People'll remember that fat arse of a poet and his *'terrible beauty'* but no one will remember the ones who died in Spain."

"I never thought I'd hear you talk like this."

Caffrey grew angry. "Look, I'm telling you this as a friend. Take their money—hand over the girl, disappear to England or somewhere until things settle down. You can't live here like Robinson Crusoe for the rest of your life. They know where you are. You're lucky they sent me out to find you."

Holland was growing heated too. He leant over, the Parabellum loose in his hand.

"Am I lucky?"

"You're a dumb fucking arsehole, Holland. I can't save you a second time."

"A second time? When the hell did you ever save me! I'm always the one pulling *you* out of scrapes."

210

Caffrey's face tightened, his eyes shone. The eyelids with the blond lashes, naked and pink, closed like lips.

"Don't you remember," he said slowly, "standing alone in a big field up against two armed men, one with a carbine? All you had was a defective handgun. How do you really think you got out of that death trap on your own? I suppose you think Jesus, Mary and all their little saints protected you?"

Holland clapped his hand on his knee. "So there *was* a sniper. I couldn't figure out how the blondie guy got a hole in his chest like that. It was an exit wound! Was it you? How could—"

"It was me. I was lying in a spider hole for over two hours. My muscles were so stiff, it's a wonder I was able to hit an elephant."

"It was all a set up then?"

"Yeah, even Farkas didn't know what was going on. It would have worked if you hadn't played the big hero and I hadn't decided to save your lousy hide."

Holland was puzzled. "You could have hit anyone in that field."

"I had a single shot Hornet. There wasn't time to reload after I downed the man with the carbine. I should have gone for the guy with the trilby first. That was the plan. He was the important one. He's the one who ratted on Farkas. This whole mess started because of your heroics. What difference did it make to you if the Hungarian got himself killed anyway?"

There was nothing Holland could say at first. "I think they were onto Farkas already." He wasn't quite sure why he had said this but he suddenly recalled the look of panic in Farkas' eyes after he received the phone call in London.

"Maybe," said Caffrey. "It's all history now. But you've got to hand over the girl. If you don't, Farkas will go to the Brits and crack this whole thing open."

"Why should I do that, even if I had her, that is?"

"Well, she's not playing with a clean deck of cards either, Holly. Why do you think she didn't go to work the morning Farkas disappeared?"

Holland twiddled with the safety catch of the Parabellum.

"And how do you think we found you? Think about it. Your little girlfriend rang her landlady in Dublin, who just happens to be on the Mundial payroll. Did she tell you that?"

"Mrs Fitzgibbons! So that's how they got to FX."

"I really didn't know about that, Holly. I'm sorry. I'm truly sorry."

Holland waved the gun at Caffrey.

"Go on back to the boat. Tell them I'll come with the girl tomorrow."

"It's the only way to get out of this," said Caffrey turning away.

"I know."

24

Holland crouched under the arch of the bridge in Abbeylara. It was five a.m., fifteen minutes before sunrise. Overhead, clouds sailed ponderously through the lightening skies, large and complex with rain. He heard a vehicle move slowly down the road. It stopped directly above his head, and over the sound of running water he could hear the engine throbbing. It was a motorcar, an expensive model and reasonably new. A door opened. There were two voices, one recognisably English.

"Y'know," the English one said, "I says to myself when I turned forty: I says, 'You've had your fucks, mate,' know what I mean? Birth, copulation and death. That's what the poets say, isn't it? You have your fucks when you're young. And then it's over."

Holland wasn't able to make out the reply, if there was one. The other man was probably standing on the far side of the car. He couldn't believe his good luck. He had expected them to park halfway between the bridge and the ruined abbey where it would have been difficult to creep up on them. His plan was simple; overpower them or kill them and then take the car.

Holland decided to take his chance now: his only hope was to attack at close range. He left the security of the arch and inched his way up the bank, holding onto the stone wall with his left hand to support himself. He stopped when he could see the roof of the car, black against the pre-dawn sky. The shape seemed familiar.

He released the safety catch of the Parabellum. Once he jumped the first man, he should be able to use the car as a shield, get in and drive off. With the gun in his left hand, he began to climb over the wall to the road; it was too high to leap over in one movement. The Parabellum scraped against the dressed stones at the top, but he had committed himself. Holland dropped down onto the road and took the first man by surprise. When he saw the gun, the man's hands automatically shot up as though through long years of practice. He was short and stocky with a round face and grey hair balding from the forehead: the car behind him was the blue Packard saloon Holland had seen in Dublin and Dun Laoghaire. Holland quickly ran his hand up and down his prisoner's chest; he didn't seem to be armed. He indicated that the bald man should lie face down. There was no sign of the second man. Perhaps he had already started walking towards the abbey? Holland could hear the shallow stream gurgle under the bridge: the noise, which normally would have sounded soothing, now seemed menacing. He placed his foot gently on the prostrate man's neck.

The man whispered: "Take it easy, son," as though the fact that Holland was holding a gun to his head put them on familiar terms. There was a sudden burst of laughter from the other side of the car.

"You should have stayed on this side, Englishman. He'll drill a hole in you for sure."

The accent was foreign: Holland thought he had heard it before. He wished he could understand the levity of the second man; why he was giving his position away. It made no sense. Fear began to stir inside him. He leant in close to the side of the car and looked through the window of the driver's seat; there was no key in the ignition. It was starting to look like a set up.

"Irishman," shouted the second man, "there is a sniper only forty yards behind you. Try to look round slowly if you wish. If you don't put down your weapon, he will surely drill a hole in your head when I raise my hand."

Holland dropped to his knees as close to the Englishman as he could get. The sweat on his forehead pricked at him like frost.

"He's not kidding," said the Englishman. "There's someone up there who wants to finish his chat with you."

Holland pressed the nose of the gun against his captive's face and turned his head. Perched above the road, beside a large rock, was a man with a rifle. He was hunched up in firing position and Holland could make out the distinct business-like lens of the telescopic sight.

"He could shoot a pimple off your chin at that range," the Englishman said.

Holland considered hiding under the car but that would simply delay the inevitable. He couldn't even use the Englishman as a shield; the sniper already had a clean shot. For a second they remained in their positions in the sleeping village, as immobile as figures in a tableau. Then Holland lowered his gun, and the Englishman whistled: a few seconds later he heard the second man move around the car. Holland put the safety catch on and handed over the Parabellum.

The Englishman sat up and took it from him.

"You could do someone an injury with one of these, mate," he said as he examined it.

Holland was shoved into the back of the Packard and the second man deftly bound his hands together with wire. Everything was suddenly very business-like, as though taking a prisoner in this way was just a normal part of their job. They waited silently while the sniper climbed carefully down from his position. Holland wasn't particularly surprised to see that it was Caffrey. The driver too was familiar. He recognised the crew cut from their trip to the Wicklow Mountains. It was Rodolf, the Dutchman with the lighter.

Caffrey got into the front passenger seat without looking once at Holland.

"Good idea with the fixed rifle, Irish," said the Englishman warmly. "You knew your man well."

"Ah sure, we had the same training," said Caffrey playing up his Irish accent. "By gob, doesn't it sit on you like an extra layer of skin."

"Start the car," the Englishman ordered. "We're too conspicuous here." Holland realised with a start that the squat, balding man beside him was their leader.

Caffrey turned round in his seat as the car veered left in the direction of FX's house. He said: "Now's the moment to tell them where the girl is, Holland."

"She's safe." Holland forced himself to smile. "And I have the papers you're looking for."

"Where?" the Englishman asked.

"Near the house."

"We were told to get the girl," the Dutchman said. "If you don't talk—"

Holland interrupted: "The girl's there too—the girl and the papers."

"You'd better not be having us on," said Caffrey, smiling. Holland felt sick just looking at him. He had a mind to say something about the oath they both had taken years back, but thought better of it.

The Englishman grinned. "I said this would be an easy assignment. All people have to do is co-operate and everything'll be cushy. That's my philosophy."

They drove through the village, past the pub-cum-shop where FX had bought his *Irish Press* every morning, and out towards the house. It was so early, there was still no sign of life in any of the buildings they passed. A cock crew far away, sounding more lost and confused than rousing. In a few minutes they were moving down the bumpy lane leading to FX's house. The Dutchman parked the car, Holland noticed, at exactly the same spot where he had seen tyre marks after FX's death. What was the point of noticing such details now, he thought to himself. There could be no hope of revenge, and there would be no one to avenge *him*.

They left the car and he led them down to the lake-shore, past the cottage and along the almost invisible path that he and Sabine had followed on their trips back and forth to the house. They walked in single file with Holland in front. Caffrey had left his sniper's rifle back in the car. The other two men were armed with revolvers. It began to drizzle. The sun made a watery appearance on the horizon.

He led them through the red bog, which glistened and sparkled under the rain, making them slip on the wet heather. Holland blinked the raindrops out of his eyes and thought morosely of Sabine, remembered putting tiny yellow asphodel flowers in her hair. Birdsong flooded the woods. He took them through the trees and thick undergrowth to the shelter. The pot was there, filled with potato peelings, beside a dead fire. It all looked small and pathetic seen with a stranger's eye. It reminded Holland of the primitive huts he had seen pictures of in Africa or the Pacific. He felt embarrassed, as though Sabine and he had been a married couple surprised by a visit from wealthy relatives.

The Englishman said: "So this is where your hidey-hole was. This close, eh. I had no idea. Where's the girl then?"

The Dutchman put his gun away and began to search behind the camp, blundering through the thick undergrowth. Caffrey stayed behind and leaned against a tree.

Holland said: "She probably heard us coming. I can show you the papers."

The Englishman was instantly suspicious. It was rather comical to observe his reaction, like watching an actor in a B-movie.

He looked with distaste at the inside of the shelter. "I hope this isn't something you've planned, mate. It'll be worse for you." He waved his revolver at Caffrey, "Better go in and take a look."

"Anything to oblige," said Caffrey in a bored voice. He came out with the satchel Holland had received from Farkas. Before making a move to open it, Caffrey looked Holland straight in the eye. Holland nodded slightly to indicate that there was no danger.

The Englishman flicked through the sheaf of papers, the gun held absent-mindedly underneath. For a second, Holland contemplated making a run for it. Caffrey didn't appear to be armed. But he realised that with his hands bound, he wouldn't get more than a few yards.

The Englishman suddenly threw the papers into the grass. "These are worthless," he screamed, "We have all these already; they're completely fucking worthless."

Even in this, thought Holland, Farkas had tricked him.

The Englishman meanwhile was working himself into a rage. "I've had about enough of this larking about. This one's never going to talk, is he?" He looked questioningly at Caffrey. "We're wasting our fucking time here, ain't we? Just getting older." He turned abruptly to Holland as though suddenly aware of his presence. "Well, you, mate, are not going to get much older."

Holland knew what was happening; it was the work-up required by some men before killing in cold blood. Holland was now the Englishman's hated enemy, able to ruin his life and blight his future. He was raping the wife and killing the children the Englishman hadn't even had yet. The Englishman cocked the revolver and raised it to point at Holland's forehead. Holland felt a great swelling sensation inside him as if some unknown component of his body had decided to announce itself. He could visualise the bullet leaving the gun and entering his brain at 1200 yards a second, atomising all love, all hope. The Englishman used both hands to steady his revolver. And then Holland's body seemed to be carried aloft in a blaze of light and fire. So it must have been in the beginning.

Caffrey shot the Englishman in the side of the head before his finger even touched the trigger. The Dutchman, no more than ten yards away, desperately began to fumble for his revolver. His hands managed to pull the gun out of the holster, almost dropping it in his haste, but it was all much too late. Caffrey had already calmly turned and walked two paces towards him. The first bullet hit him square in the middle of the chest and knocked him over. Then Caffrey walked up and finished him with a shot to the head. After he had done this, Caffrey's arm dropped and he sank to his knees. Birds screamed and screeched from the lake. Ducks blundered panic-stricken across the surface and into the sky, and a grebe dived gracefully beneath the surface.

"Well," said Caffrey slowly, "I guess this is the end of my collaboration with Mundial."

"It is for them anyway," said Holland, astonished to hear the sound of his own voice. Everything around him had taken on a woolly appearance, as though the colours had been mixed differently. It was hard to believe he was still alive. In front of him lay the Englishman, his head smashed open, blood and brain matter on the grass sward.

"How well did you know these characters?" he asked.

Caffrey looked round distractedly. It took him a second to reply.

"Not very well. The Dutchman was one of Dr Mahr's recruits, a real fanatic. I was told his job was to bully the Germans living here to join the Nazi party."

"And the Englishman?"

"His name's Alf Repton. He wasn't political at all; he didn't even know what Mundial was about. Was just in it for the money. A bit of a gardening enthusiast. Always going on about what he would plant when he settled down. Much good it'll do him now. We'll need to get rid of these bodies. You might as well call your little woman. These two aren't going to do her any harm now."

"She's not here."

Caffrey jerked himself to his feet. "What!"

"I got her to take FX's boat over to the barracks in Finea. I thought it was the safest place."

Caffrey was suddenly furious. He shouted at Holland: "That's informing, or fucking damn close to it. If McDaid knew, he'd have your head."

"That's rich coming from you, Caffrey. What rule haven't you broken?"

"I never once even came close to betraying the Movement. Never."

"Look, we'll get rid of the bodies. I know a good place for them. No digging required. After that, we'll see if we can pick up Sabine. She wasn't going to tell them anything much; just that she was Farkas' secretary and in fear of her life. She won't mention either you or me. If she does, I'll plug her myself."

Caffrey whooped. He came over to Holland and held him by the shoulders.

"Me ould bold Holly is back. Oh I could kiss you, boy."

"In my present condition, that would be grounds for rape proceedings. Come on, get these wires off my hands."

Caffrey unwound the wires on his wrists, and Holland rubbed the skin vigorously. "I was beginning to lose all feeling in my fingers."

"You could have lost a lot more feeling than that. You're lucky I had this in my pocket." He handed Holland the handgun. "It's a Walther. I got it off the fellow I shot in England."

Holland weighed it in his hand in wonderment. It was small and light, like a toy. He gave it back to Caffrey.

"Let's move these bodies."

Caffrey examined Holland's jacket and trousers. They were torn and streaked with dried mud.

"Have you no other clothes. You could—"

"I know what you're going to say. But no way am I getting into a dead man's clothes."

"The Dutchman's about your size, a bit bigger in the shoulders maybe."

"I still have the suit Farkas bought me."

They dragged the bodies to an area of swamp between the red bog and a desolate section of the Inny, close to where the river emptied out of the lake. At the edge of the swamp was a stand of Yellow Flags whose long, sword-like leaves shimmered and made elegant gestures when disturbed.

Holland and Caffrey rested. Then they went though the pockets of the dead men and took whatever money they could find.

It was a poor haul. Holland caught Caffrey's eye. "They weren't going to pay me £500, were they?"

"You'd have got it if you'd played your cards better. But you're right; they didn't have that kind of money with them."

Holland encountered a cold metallic object in one of the Dutchman's pockets and he pulled out his souvenir lighter from the war. It reminded him that he badly needed a cigarette. But first they had work to do. They grasped the Englishman by the legs, swung him, and then when the momentum was sufficient, let go. The body dived in an arc into the bile-green centre of the swamp and sank within seconds. The Dutchman was heavier and more difficult to swing but they managed to heave him in close to the centre too. His body wallowed on the surface for about a minute, long enough for them to worry that he wouldn't sink, his arms moving in remarkably lifelike poses like an uncertain swimmer—so much so that Holland feared that he wasn't quite dead—and then he too sank. His left hand was the last part of him to disappear; it pointed upwards in a relaxed, philosophical manner before vanishing into the mud.

They watched all this in silence. Then, when it was over, Caffrey passed a packet of Woodbines to Holland and Holland lit their cigarettes with the Dutchman's lighter.

The bodies had created a large muddy stain, streaked in places by blood, in the middle of the swamp.

"The plants will have grown over that in a week or so," Holland said.

Caffrey nodded as he sucked on his cigarette. The sight of the sinking bodies had dampened his normally high spirits. The rapidity of it, especially, had got to him. The bodies hadn't even had the chance to get cold before the earth had claimed them.

"If they ever find those two, they'll probably think they had been riding around with Cúchulainn."

Huge bubbles, probably air from the men's lungs, burst the surface of the mud pool.

They returned to the grove. While Holland changed his clothes, Caffrey covered what stains there were with leaves and branches from the shelter and collected the spent cartridges. He burnt the papers Farkas had given Holland. The spirits could now return to this place, thought Holland, the spirits and the wild animals. With Sabine gone, it had lost all human significance for him.

They trudged back to the car. It began to rain again. They crossed the shoreline, the waters of the lake agitated by tiny explosions from the sky, and Caffrey pointed at some footmarks on the ground. "Four sets out, two sets back."

Holland looked at him with warmth. "I forgot to say—thanks for, you know...."

Caffrey smiled: "The funny thing is, Repton had fought in the trenches. Went over to France when he was seventeen. Survived the whole bloody war without a scratch. He was lucky, he said, never took any chances. What he didn't understand was that *here*, in this country, everything is personal, including killing."

Holland thought about the herds of Russian soldiers Farkas had described, men running to their deaths without rifles or even boots on their feet.

At the car, Caffrey extracted the Parabellum from under the backseat where the Englishman had hidden it and handed it to Holland. They drove back to Abbeylara, past the high Gothic tower of the abbey, eternally besieged by an army of granite headstones, and took the road to Finea. As usual, the village looked trim, tranquil and devoid of life. Caffrey parked the car on the lane leading down to the landing place. There was no sign of FX's boat. Holland got out and checked the other side of the bridge while Caffrey remained behind on guard.

He returned after a few minutes. Caffrey looked at him questioningly.

"She might have beached it on the lake and walked up. She's not used to rowing and there is a current."

They sat in the car and discussed what to do. The village was gradually coming to life around them. A postman cycled by and a farmer with a cartload of hay drove past.

"Jaysus, it's like one of those documentaries about rural Ireland. All I'm waiting for is the commentary." He stopped talking, surprised that Holland wasn't listening. "God, you have it bad. You really want to get hold of that little woman, don't you?"

Holland remained silent. He could imagine Sabine capsizing on the lake, calling for help with no one near enough to hear her.

"I could go in and ask about fishing rights or something? With an English accent," Caffrey suggested.

"If Sabine's there—"

"You said she wouldn't mention us, remember?"

Gentle white puffs of smoke began to emerge from the chimney of the police barracks. "It looks safe enough to me. They're probably inside drinking tea and discussing the danger to their manhood of the high saddle."

"Take your short-arm just in case. I'll keep the engine running."

Caffrey walked up the path to the main door and disappeared round the side. Holland lit up one of the cigarettes he had left behind and checked the Parabellum. He didn't have long to wait. Caffrey returned as sprightly as when he went in.

"I don't think she's in there. There was only one guard I could see and he looked as if I'd just woken him up."

Both men were famished. Caffrey went into the only shop in the village and bought bread, cheese and a bottle of lemonade. They wolfed down the food, biting off the cheese in mouthfuls. Then, in the middle of eating a large chunk of bread, Holland suddenly stopped. He remembered that he hadn't seen any food in the shelter when they'd left it. Sabine must have taken it with her. He said nothing, but Caffrey seemed to sense that something was bothering him.

"Are you sure she was a real woman and not a little elf or something? Maybe she's gone back to her own people in one of those fairy forts."

"You're just a cynical jackeen," Holland said.

"You really have no idea where she is?"

"No. But I have an idea where she'll be heading: Derry, Glasgow, London."

"Derry, for Christ's sake! How will she get there without a vehicle?"

"We were going to drive up there in the Wolseley. It's parked near here."

"Christ! That's it then! She's probably there waiting for you."

Strangely, the same thought had not occurred to Holland. He wondered whether it was because he knew her too well: Sabine would either do exactly as he asked her or something completely different. Caffrey threw the rest of the food into the backseat and started the car. Holland directed him over the bridge and then right, down the pot-holed boreen, which went past the bog.

As they bumped along, Holland said: "How are you going to explain the dead men to McDaid? He'll have a fit."

"I'll tell him some cock-and-bullshit story about you outdrawing them, and then sparing my miserable life."

"Don't make it too elaborate."

"Don't worry, I won't. What are you going to do? You'll need to get away from here."

"I thought I'd drive to Derry, take the ferry to Glasgow and then head for London. There are millions of Paddies down there: they'll never find me. Maybe I can borrow some of your petrol?"

"Sure. There's a couple of extra gallons in the boot."

Within a few minutes the Packard was bucking up and down on the tiny track leading to the lake. Holland showed Caffrey where he'd hidden the Wolseley and he parked beside it. They got out and wandered around the clearing. There was no sign of Sabine. They waited in silence and finished another cigarette. Clouds broke apart and sharp beams of light lit up the lake. Caffrey drummed his fingers on the outside of the car. It was warm from the heat of the sun. He was agitated. His face was set hard, from thinking—or from a nagging problem—it was difficult to say which. Then without any warning, in one single movement, he thrust his hand into his pocket and pulled out the Walther. He pointed the gun at Holland. But Holland had read him well and stood barely twenty yards away holding the Parabellum.

"I have to take you back to McDaid, Holly."

"I don't think so."

"This is fucking ridiculous! I don't want to do this.... If we'd found the girl, I could have let you go, but—"

"Don't do it then. Let me go: you're a free man."

"You know, Holly, I'm not. My soul is pawned to the Movement, remember?"

"I'll shoot, or be shot. You won't take me back."

Caffrey smiled bitterly. "I took the precaution of emptying your magazine when you went down to the boats. I'm sorry."

"Do you think I don't know when the magazine is full or empty? I put in the extra rounds I had in my pocket."

Holland fully expected Caffrey to lower his gun and allow him to leave. But Caffrey fired. The first bullet grazed Holland's ear, the second ripped through his jacket between the arm and the chest. Holland aimed instinctively and pulled the trigger. The gun bucked, for an instant alive. Afterwards Holland couldn't remember anything but the recoil. The heavy Parabellum bullet entered Caffrey's chest below his raised right arm. His body crumpled up and dropped to the ground. An awful silence occupied the clearing. Holland threw down his gun and ran over. He took Caffrey in his arms. It was impossible to staunch the blood. All colour left Caffrey's face, his eyes glazed over. Holland spoke tenderly as if to a child. "Don't go, Conall, don't go on me. I didn't want to do this. You made me shoot; you made me shoot! You'd cry for me, Conall, you'd fucking cry for me."

Caffrey's right eyelid flickered, the lips moved as if to speak, but when Holland felt for a pulse there was nothing.

After he had recovered a little he whispered in Irish, *Go ndéanaidh Dia trócaire ar a anam*, May God have mercy on his soul. Then he gently closed the flickering eye with his finger, the pale eyelash moth-like against his skin.

He laid Caffrey's body on the ground and went down to the lakeshore to wash his head and his hands. There was some blood on his ear where Caffrey's bullet had nicked him. But when he licked it off his hand, he didn't taste his own blood; he tasted Sabine.

The world had changed utterly and was still the same. It was a surprise for him to see the same hills hanging over the lake, the same birds bobbing up and down in the water far away, the same unreachable islands. He went back to Caffrey's body, took off his jacket and pocketed his money and personal things. When the time was right, he would send them to his family. His heart was intolerably full as though it had doubled in size inside his chest, but he forced himself to keep thinking out his escape. He opened the boot of the Packard and found two shovels and a can of petrol. At the edge of the bog where the soil was soft, he dug a shallow grave. Then he dragged Caffrey's body over and rolled it gently inside but could not bear to cover him. The blood on Caffrey's clothes was already turning black.

He muttered to the corpse: "'We're all the same dead', Caff, as you used to say."

But he would not say that, or anything else, again, thought Holland. He sat by the side of the grave for half an hour smoking and watching the face of his friend. Then he placed the sniper's rifle beside Caffrey's body and the Walther in his hand, as though he were an ancient warrior. He picked up the shovel and covered him with the red peaty earth. When he was finished filling in the grave, he concealed it with leaves and branches and returned to the cars.

He took one of the containers from the boot of the Packard and emptied the petrol into the Wolseley. Then he got into the Packard and started the engine. He smoked a cigarette and sat thinking, his arms resting on the driving wheel. The Parabellum still lay on the ground where he had dropped it. He picked it up—it seemed heavier in his hand—and walked down to the shore. A cormorant flew low over the water, making him think of the sea. But this was not the sea.

Holland cast the Parabellum as far into Lough Sheelin as he could. In a great curve it travelled into the sky, making one last attempt to translate its surface into light, before disappearing beneath the waters of the lake.

He went back to the Wolseley and threw a lighted match into the front seat. The flames were red and blue behind him as he drove away in the other car.

25

It took Holland nearly four days to reach London. The first part of the journey was the riskiest. He wasn't more than a mile inside Northern Ireland before he was stopped by the RUC. He showed them a triptyque that he had found in the glove compartment. Luckily, it had been properly stamped by the Irish customs and they let him go after paying a small fine. He left the Packard in the centre of Derry. The ferry crossing to Glasgow passed without incident and there was no security on the other side. He took the train to London, but was unable to sleep. During the journey, his anger at Sabine's disappearance turned into an aching sense of his own loss.

As soon as he arrived in London, without ever making a conscious decision about it, he began to search for her. He tried checking the telephone books but there was no one of that name inside. He walked randomly through the streets looking for any clue to her whereabouts, barely aware that he was in the second largest city in the world.

After a few days he found the Mundial offices in Soho but the sign had been replaced by one advertising a company dealing in ladies' hosiery and undergarments. In the newspapers he read about the discovery of a major German spy ring. The spies were expelled but there was no information about how they had been caught. He wondered whether Farkas had spilled the beans, but there was no way for him to check without endangering himself. He could not go to the authorities and he stayed away from anyone connected to the Movement.

Within a fortnight he ran out of money. He had to leave the boarding house he had been staying at and spent his last few shillings in a pub called the Rose and Crown which was frequented by the Irish. There, he was befriended by some navvies who got him fixed up with a contractor. He began to work; mind-numbing labour, digging trenches for the gas company. Labouring emptied his mind of Sabine and in the evenings he drank heavily, which served the same purpose. Weeks passed. Occasionally, he was persuaded to go to one of the Irish clubs. Drink was not served inside but the navvies, mostly big silent men from the west of Ireland, managed to get drunk anyway. Some of the young women took an interest in him but he avoided any involvement. It was dangerous to give anything away and he was not really interested. Sabine had spoiled him: he looked at these young women, in their cheap dresses and Woolworth's perfume, and he could only see how different they were to her.

The weather grew colder. He worked nearly sixty hours a week and drank most of the money he earned. Sometimes he got into a fight. The world seemed to have ended for him.

One day, when he was wandering back to his digs from a pub, he took a wrong turning and ended up in Knightsbridge. He was suddenly blinded by a bright light. A large car pulled up beside him on the kerb and a chauffeur hopped out. There were three toffs inside. Holland recognised the last man. He was a little fatter than Holland remembered him and his hair was greyer but he was sure who it was. Holland walked over as determinedly as he could, the drink swilling around in his body, making him unsteady. The chauffeur blocked his way.

"I know that man," Holland said thickly. "I need to speak to him."

The chauffeur laughed. "Go on, Paddy, pull the other one: this is no place for the likes of you."

Holland remained standing, one hand raised. The chauffeur tried to grab his arm to push him away, but all the frustrations and humiliations of the last months had built up to the point where Holland could only react in one way. He struck out, but his punch missed its target by six inches and he found himself lying on the pavement, the chauffeur's foot pressed down on his chest. His rage could not help him. He cried out like a wounded animal.

"What shall I do with him, sir?" the chauffeur asked.

Holland became aware of the group of men standing around him, viewing him as some sort of specimen, the violent and irrational Celt.

One of the toffs said: "How frightfully grim. Shall we call a policeman?"

He could hear Mr Greene's voice, unruffled and soothing in the background. Then his face leant over him, so close that Holland could feel his breath tickle his ear.

"I'm afraid I hardly recognised you, my friend. I'm giving you a little something. Come and visit me if you wish." He placed some money in the pocket of Holland's jacket and the boot was removed. When he stood up, Mr Greene and the toffs had disappeared. Only the chauffeur remained, posed like Mussolini, with folded arms and legs apart.

"Go on home, Paddy, if you remember where it is. You're lucky I don't break your miserable Irish neck."

Under the light of a streetlamp, Holland examined what Mr Greene had given him. Wrapped around a ten-shilling note was his business card.

Holland took the following day off work—which meant that he was docked a week's wages—but he didn't care. He couldn't wait. He had to know about Sabine. Greene's offices were in the City near Lincoln's Inn. Holland walked past the most expensive tailoring shops in London, togged out in a shabby and torn suit and workman's boots, and, as usual, hatless. As he expected, he did not get past the ground floor front desk. At first they told him that Mr Greene was away on business, but he waved the business card and insisted that they ring his number. A blonde secretary, whose clothes and demeanour reminded him painfully of Sabine, came down in a lift to fetch him. They ascended to the third floor and there she left him alone in an office lined with files and legal tomes. He took a seat and waited. For the first time in months, the voices in his head were still. There had been a purpose in his returning to this city.

Mr Greene walked in and sat down. He placed his elbows on the desk and joined his hands together as if to pray.

"What can I do for you, Mr Byrne?"

"You can call me Holland. It's my real name."

"Does it really matter, my friend? One eventually forgets all the real names and all the aliases."

"Where's Farkas?"

Greene rubbed his forehead wearily. "He's in a safe place. The truth is, he was forced to, you might say, realign his allegiance. But in the end he did not let down his clients."

"Men died. Did you know that?"

"It was all very regrettable. I'm afraid I do not know much more than what was written in the newspapers. Anyway, I was wondering whether you needed a little help, something financial? Or I could see if I could find you a position. You were an excellent chauffeur."

Holland was immediately wary. "Why should you bother helping me?"

Greene smiled. "I've heard reports about you. You're a good person. I would like to help."

"Would this have anything to do with Sabine?"

"I'm not at liberty to say."

"Can I ask if she's alive?"

Greene's eyes gazed off into the distance. He folded his hands again and the silence was so long that Holland wondered if he had heard the question.

"Let us say that Sabine is alive and in good health."

"How did she get away? Did you—"

"No. She was very resourceful. She took a boat down the river you'd told her about. The Inn?"

"The Inny."

"She had some food with her. She kept to the shore during the day and rowed at night. It was a very thinly populated area and she had a good map, she told me. The current helped, of course."

"How far did she get?"

"She rowed across a large lake and then hitched a lift to a town called Athlone. She was half-starved but asked the locals if there was a Jewish family in the town, and so there was. They took her in and looked after her until we could send her some money."

"And who are 'we'?"

"Let us just say that we are an organisation that looks after Jews. She was able to get in touch with some mutual acquaintances in London, and they contacted me."

"And where is she now?"

"We sent her some papers. Sabine took a plane from Dublin to Bristol, and we got her a cabin on a liner to New York."

Holland paused. "And what about Farkas? What happened to him?"

"He co-operated with the authorities. He was very helpful, you understand. It was part of the deal."

"So he made a deal with the authorities here?"

Greene stared out the window: "I shouldn't really be telling you all this, but I'm a sentimental man and I feel you deserve to know. When put to the test, Farkas couldn't leave his clients in the lurch. He remembered his duty to them. You understand all about duty, don't you?" Greene stood up as though their interview had terminated. "Mr Holland, we all owe you a debt, especially Sabine. A great debt. Why don't you let me arrange a job for you? I have many contacts." Greene reached for a chequebook in his jacket. "I can help you with some money now if you need it. We can call it a loan—"

"I'd rather have Sabine's address."

Greene withdrew his hand from his jacket and began to fidget nervously with a cigar box.

"You're annoyed with her. I understand that. It's regrettable but I'm—"

"You've got it wrong. I just want to see her again."

Greene retook his seat. He extracted a cigar from the box and twiddled with it for a moment. He passed it under his nose and closed his eyes. "My doctor has told me to stay off these. But he hasn't said I can't imagine a smoke or enjoy watching someone else smoke. Could I tempt you? They're the best quality Havana cigars." Holland shook his head. Greene continued: "Sabine is a very special young woman but—"

"But not for the likes of me."

"She's putting together a new life for herself, in America. Last I heard, she was engaged to be married... to a magnate of some kind."

The word 'magnate' made a jarring note in Holland's head. It sounded as if Greene had just made it up. For the first time in the conversation, Holland began to feel that he had the advantage.

"Well, Mr Greene, if she is so well established, as you say, then it can hardly do her any harm to receive a letter from an old friend. I might even look her up. I've considered emigrating to America myself."

Greene smiled sadly. "A letter from you is the last thing she needs. The poor girl had a—you might say—a bad attack of nerves. I'm afraid it wouldn't be healthy for her to be reminded of her time in Ireland."

"She's in England, isn't she? Probably here in London."

Greene stopped fiddling with the cigar, stopped moving altogether. His voice changed. It took on a harsher edge.

"Mr Holland, you can have £100 for your trouble if you leave this minute. I will only require a receipt from you," he said, his eyes averted.

"I could mention the fact that Farkas is still alive to a few of my friends. You've probably heard about how Republicans treat people who double-cross them."

Greene smiled expansively as if they were talking humorously. "And I'm sure Farkas could have you and your friends put away for a very long time too. He knows everything—all about the sharpshooter Mundial employed for instance."

"The sniper is dead. At least five men are dead because of Farkas."

"Ah," said Greene. "That's very unfortunate but I don't like threats, my friend. I'm not in the business of threatening people or being threatened. Here I am trying to help you and you repay me like this. That's not very fair, is it?"

Holland placed his hands on the desk. Its surface felt remarkably smooth under his calloused fingers. "I don't want to threaten anyone either. All I'm asking is that you contact Sabine and tell her I want to see her. She decides. If she doesn't want to see me, that's all right. She can write you a note. I know her handwriting."

Greene leant back in his chair as though to view Holland anew. "You are quite sincere about this, aren't you?"

Holland nodded.

"I can't promise you anything, but let us say that that you come back in three days."

26

Early November 1937, late evening. Holland took the Underground and then began to walk. It was cold, a drier more clinical cold than that he was used to in Ireland. He stopped at a street lamp and consulted the London A-Z. His finger traced a path through the labyrinth. He walked past street after street, seeing nothing, not registering the freezing wind, not responding to the darkness pressing hard on every side, trying not to listen to the harsh words whispering in his own mind. Words that prepare you for failure, words that try to keep you on your feet when your whole future has crumbled and fallen away. How could he know whether or not she would even want to see him again, her wild man from the Irish interior? For all he knew, he could be walking into a trap. Greene had simply given him an address and a time. It was the classic decoy and ambush scenario.

The streets fell away. His footsteps echoed behind him as though they belonged to someone else. Following him this time, there were no shadowy figures, no men with guns. All there was was his past, frozen like a lake in winter, the sedge withered.

He arrived at the address, a Georgian building not unlike Mrs Fitzgibbons' house in Rathmines. Holland was momentarily at a loss. He saw the name Greene had given him beside the bell: Samantha Blake, her own first name changed, and her mother's surname anglicised, to keep away unwanted visitors. Was he also one of these undesirables? He could not ring, not yet.

He skirted around the building, his years of training returning like an extra sense, and entered the garden at the back. She was living on the ground floor. There was a light on somewhere inside, refracted through the back window from a place deep inside the flat. He moved behind some bushes to watch. Minutes passed. His feet began to grow cold but he hardly noticed. Suddenly there was a movement in one of the windows. A light went on. For a second he was mesmerised. He could see the side of her face illuminated by a naked bulb; her dark hair was cut shorter, the curve of her neck more exposed.

He decided to leave the safety of his hiding place, and go to the front door. After he had rung the bell, his body was filled with a sense of serenity: as though he had become separated from the world and was at last floating free. A door opened inside the building. Music wafted out, from a gramophone or wireless, the words hard to identify. Footsteps.

The door opened quickly and he suddenly stood face to face with Sabine. She was wearing a print dress and a large grey cardigan she hugged close to her body. She seemed more petite, more fragile than he remembered. They stood there not saying anything, waiting—it seemed—for some exterior event to jog them into action.

Sabine was the first to break the silence. "I've been expecting you," she said. "Come in."

Holland obeyed, following her through the hall and into her flat.

"It's a small place, but I like it." She looked at him again and smiled shyly. The light spread tiny dark angles over her face, which was paler and more drawn than during the summer. She shut the door and showed him into a small living room. The only illumination came from an articulated table lamp on a desk. He could see paintings on the wall and a well-stocked bookcase. There was a faint scent of perfume, and, somewhere in the background, Sabine's own personal scent.

"Please sit down," she said.

Holland moved over to a sofa covered with a blue rug. He was painfully aware that he had yet to open his mouth. He fought for something to say.

Finally he said: "I've been looking for you."

"I know." She walked over to the gramophone and lifted the needle, stopping the music. "Henry Purcell."

"I knew a Purcell in the Movement."

Sabine sat down on a wooden chair in front of the desk.

"Have you been keeping well?" Her voice sounded distant. Holland could feel despair clutching at him. He ran his fingers through his hair and forced himself to take a deep breath. He made himself smile but felt his face produce a grimace instead.

"Sabine, we're not old school friends. What happened?"

Her head fell forward. She rubbed her eyes. He could not tell if tears or laughter were welling up inside her. "I didn't know how to tell you, Holland. I felt so guilty."

"You don't have to feel guilty. You saved yourself."

"I just left you. I followed the river from that map of your uncle's. I let the flow of the water lead me away. For such a long time I convinced myself that you were dead."

"Sometimes, I thought I *was* dead."

"That time, Holland, is gone. It was special, at the lake, but everything is different now."

"You've found somebody else?"

"No. There's nobody else. Do you know, I was sure I was pregnant when I got back to England. I really was convinced I was carrying the baby of a dead IRA man."

Holland smiled. "There's still time."

She looked at him, scrutinised his face to see if he was joking. "For a long time I felt shame. Do you understand?"

"Why?"

She paused, then said: "Your uncle. You. All the ones who died because of me. I was the informer, you see. I'm the reason Farkas had to disappear."

Holland sat back in the sofa. "I don't get it."

"I'm the one who told the Zionists about what was going on at Mundial. I found out months ago that German intelligence were running the place. I opened a letter by mistake at the office and I began to put the rest of it together. I'm responsible. How many are dead?"

"Five I know of."

"I would do it again, Holland. You must hate me?" Holland shook his head. "What about you? Mr Greene didn't tell me how you got away."

"Sometimes I wondered, did I get away…." He stopped himself, and then continued. "Caffrey saved my life. He was a good friend in the end."

He couldn't tell her the truth about Caffrey. Not yet.

"You know, Farkas went to the authorities here, as soon as he knew I was safe. He was given a guarantee that I would be allowed to stay in Britain. The Germans were expelled and the Mundial operation was closed down. They couldn't find one of the operatives, a sharpshooter."

Holland recalled Caffrey's face before he covered it with earth.

"There are people after me too," he said, "but the trail's dead now. I bought another man's identity. It's common practice here with the navvies, to get the dole money. The other fella gave me his papers and went back to Ireland."

"So what's your new name?"

"Bradley. John Bradley. I forget which county I'm from. Donegal I think."

"Come here, John."

She unfolded her arms and he went over to where she was sitting. He sank to his knees and buried his face in her belly. Her warmth filled him. She wrapped her arms around him. No words were said.